THEIR STAR IS THEIR WORLD

D.M. Herrmann

Praise for *Innisfree: Book One of the John Henry Chronicles*

"*Innisfree* is an interesting read, and a fairly accurate portrayal of human nature in extreme circumstances. Set in current times, with much of the unrest of the world today, D.M. Herrmann captures a possible future for us."

—Brian Oppermann, U.S. Marine Corps Combat Veteran of Desert Storm/Desert Shield

"*Innisfree* confronts the terrifying reality of a world without the conveniences we've so heavily relied upon and just how far you would go to protect your family. This novel will keep you reading until the very end, securing its place among the top necessities you would grab if the world were to crumble."

—Callie Trautmiller, Author of *Becoming American*

THEIR STAR IS THEIR WORLD

Book Two of the
John Henry Chronicles

D.M. Herrmann

Green Bay, WI 54311

Publisher/Executive Editor: Brittiany Koren
Cover Art Designer: Ed Vincent/ENC Graphics
Print Interior Layout Designer: Katy Brunette
Ebook Interior Layout Designer: Maria Connor
Category: Post-apocalyptic Military Fiction

Description: As the second installment in the John Henry Chronicles continues, the Henry family learns to live in a post-apocalyptic world.

Hard Cover ISBN: 978-1-951375-32-4

Paperback ISBN: 978-1-951375-33-1

Ebook ISBN: 978-1-951375-34-8

LOC Catalogue Data: Applied for.

First Edition published by Written Dreams Publishing in October, 2020.

Green Bay, WI 54311

Books by D.M. Herrmann

Innisfree, Book One in the John Henry
Chronicles
Their Star Is Their World, Book Two in the John
Henry Chronicles

Books written as Evan Michael Martin

Sorceress Rising, Book 1, A Clio Boru Story
Sorceress Revealed, Book 2, A Clio Boru Story
Sorceress Resurrected, Book 3, A Clio Boru
Story

Note from the Author

This is a work of fiction, or is it? Much of what you will read is either true or fact. Of course, the characters and the storyline are not real people.

The story contains information that anyone wanting to be prepared for an apocalyptic event could use, but that isn't the main purpose of this story. The story is about people. People who call themselves family. More than biological family, it is about how people can come together and *become* family. Through deed and circumstance, they form a bond.

This is the story of one such man and his family. Divorced and living apart from his family, he struggles during a time of enormous crisis to bring them together, keep them together, and protect them. He longs for peace, and the dream of a forest glade, where he is safe, and so are they. He faces the reality of great evil and the natural tendencies of man. This is the struggle of all who cherish their families; this is the struggle of John Henry.

This book is dedicated to families, families together, families apart, families created by circumstance. Families drawn together for good and bad; families driven apart because of words. Families reunited because of hurt. Cherish your family, regardless of where you are. Our family is the very root of our existence.

Some may find parts of the story disturbing. It should be. However, all of the so-called experts agree that our civilization on any given day is about three days away from completely breaking down *if* the right circumstances occur. The inability to provide the necessities of life will quickly degenerate, and as animals that humans are, the violent tendencies we all naturally have will return if for no other reason than to survive.

Unlike some books in this genre, this story contains profanity. I felt it was a more accurate portrayal of life in stressful times and did not want to paint an inaccurate or unrealistic picture of the environment. Much of what you can learn in this book can be put to use to help your family survive, and possibly thrive, in any short or long-term breakdown of essential services or society. We've seen this type of breakdown following natural disasters, both the good and the bad tendencies of humans.

I hope you enjoy the story, enjoy the determination, will, and struggle these characters show to survive during challenging, terrible times. In the words of one of my favorite childhood cartoon characters… "Let's get dangerous!"

—D.M. Herrmann

"...What matter to me if their star is a world?"

—Robert Browning

To L.H., thank you for kickstarting me and helping me finish this.

This "Project" is done because you believed.

Prologue

"And where were you two all day?" the young, scolding female voice asked from across the barn. "Ma was looking for you, and you were nowhere to be found."

"We were working, sweetie," the older man of the two said. The twinkle in his eyes and the smile that came through his thick beard told otherwise.

"And just what were you *working* on? I saw you put the fishing poles away."

"Busted," the other man said. The two men burst out into laughter. "Now, sweetie, we were fishing."

"Uh, huh," she replied. Skepticism was in her tone as she placed her hands on her hips. She continued, now with an accusatory tone. "I don't see any fish."

"They weren't biting," both men responded at once. The conspiratorial glance between them caused them each to take a breath. "They weren't biting, and we didn't catch any," the younger of the two men said.

"All day?" she questioned.

"Now, sweetie, it takes patience to fish, and you have to sit still."

"More like being still and napping," she said. "You gonna finish the story?"

"Story?" the man asked.

"From last night, the story, the one about my grandpa…"

***

The middle school on Stewart Avenue was bustling with activity. Black HMMWVs drove through the parking lot past the sandbag tower across from the entrance to Marathon County Park, where another tall sandbagged tower guarded its entrance. The school was now administrative offices and barracks for the Wisconsin National Guard and FEMA personnel that worked and lived there. The entries, all secured by armed guards, darkly foreshadowed the work being conducted inside. A woodland camouflaged Hummer drove through the circular drive in front of the entrance to the school-turned-headquarters. Rolling to a stop, the Hummer's passenger door opened, and a tall Native American man in a Multicam Army Combat Uniform commonly called an ACU, stepped out onto the walkway leading to the front door.

First, Sergeant Chris Rahn put his service cap on and stood still. Letting his eyes take in the scene around him, he was struck by how a middle school for kids was now a bustling military operation.

He turned a full 360 degrees, taking in everything his eyes could capture. Letting his eyes focus on Marathon County Park across the street, he saw the guard tower, unrolled strands of concertina wire in front of a tall chain-link fence surrounding the full perimeter and the roving foot patrols. Shaking his head slowly and looking at the ground, he spit, the disgust of what he saw plainly evident on his face.

Turning once again to face the door to the school, he stepped off with his left foot, a habit inherent in all who served in the U.S. Military, and purposefully walked toward the door.

The Marathon County Fairgrounds was so different from just a few short months ago. The spacious grounds, approximately six acres, were no longer a place where families came to enjoy the shade-covered tables for picnics. or outdoor fun without leaving town. Its huge red-roofed barn was now a collection of offices and other spaces to support the refugees inside. Besides the guard tower, the main entrance on

Stewart Avenue was surrounded by sandbags, behind which FEMA Guards armed with a tripod-mounted M-60 machine gun watched anyone approaching through eyes covered by dark sunglasses. A series of concrete barriers supported by movable modular vehicle barriers slowed any vehicle traffic to a slow crawl, forcing them to snake their way down the long drive. If they went right, the road took them to a dirt parking area, the bleachers and outdoor performance arena, the barn, and the exhibition buildings alongside. The grassy area beyond the arena was next to the rail line. Fenced in by rolls of concertina wire, a large number of Conex containers held the supplies for the park. The tree-covered picnic areas were still there, no longer used by visitors.

Here and there, a few black-clad guards and ACU wearing soldiers lounged, smoking while on break from their many duties. Closer to the barn and other buildings, grey jumpsuited people walked about, none for leisure as they were watched closely by an armed guard. This was one of three such facilities in the immediate Wausau, Wisconsin area. Two others existed, utilizing separate high school campuses. The campuses, classrooms, assembly areas, and cafeterias, as well as fenced-in athletic fields, made them ideal for a new purpose.

Rahm entered the school and headed straight for the main office. As he entered, he saw Major Elias Wolfe stepping out of one of the offices; a manila folder clutched in his hand. Wolfe didn't see Rahn at first.

"Major," Rahn announced.

"Yes, First Sergeant?"

"I need to speak with you, sir."

The bluntness in Rahn's tone caused Elias to raise an eyebrow. "I'm busy, First Sergeant."

"I need to see you, Sir," Rahn replied firmly.

"Have a seat, First Sergeant; I'll be with you in a moment."

Knowing that if he pushed the issue harder, he would be on the brink of insubordination, Rahn sat in one of the hard plastic and metal chairs along the wall. *Asshole.*

Chapter 1

"Loyalty, that is the strength of a family. It is just as strong, if not stronger, than the strength of an army."

—John Henry

When I first moved to Lake View, Wisconsin, I came here looking for some peace. I thought I had found it, but that was not to be. My name is John Henry, and my story continues…

I was looking for an early summer morning before the sun brightened the earth, that was the time when I liked sitting on my porch. The mosquitoes had already departed, and all that was left were a few crickets, the early bird seeking the worm, and the few nightbirds finishing up their hunt. The morning was a peaceful time, a time when I could gather my thoughts, solve my problems of which now there were many, and get my head right for the day ahead.

The chair creaked as I settled into it, a steaming cup of coffee in my hand that I rested on the chair arm. As usual, I wore my old school LL Bean heavy leather hiking boots and jeans. I'd put on a brown pocketed t-shirt today because it seemed to fit me better; I'd lost some weight. Max, King, and Grady joined me, their nails clicking on the porch boards as they wandered. Then, an oomph followed by a sigh as they settled down and went back to sleep. The life of a dog was so hard.

I stretched my jean-covered legs out in front of me, brought the cup to my mouth, taking in the awesome aroma, and sipped. The warmth went through me quickly as it made its way to my stomach. Summer mornings in Wisconsin, while not cold, could be enjoyable. The warmth of the coffee was a comfort that made this time perfect. I had to shift a bit as the holster with my Glock 19 pushed into my side. Moving the holster slightly, I settled in for my alone morning time.

Since the battle with the looter's things had been calm, Nancy was awake now, and while struggling with a few things, she was able to get out of bed and take care of almost all of her personal needs. Carol and Donna did a great job of nursing her back to health and making sure she recovered. It had been touch and go for a while, and without the technology of modern medicine, we were all scared.

It was still amazing to me was that Donna and Carol got along so well. It was no longer a secret that Carol and I were a thing. For the sake of privacy, we shared a room together; actually, we shared a bed. My concern about some cattiness between them never materialized, and for that, I was grateful. They were two incredible women.

Brian and Craig had become much closer as brothers, with Mike attaching himself quite strongly to them both. At times, I thought Brian was a bit jealous with all of the "Uncle Craig said this" and "Uncle Craig did that." He never let on, and I think Craig enjoyed the attention and bit of idol worship.

It was Craig I worried about the most. Ever since the night back in Appleton, he had adapted to this new crueler environment too easily. The violence seemed a matter of fact to him. When I tried to talk to him about it, he good-naturedly blamed video games. "Dad," he said, "it's all those violent games I play. Master Chief, Soap, Jackson, and I have taken out more bad guys than you could ever imagine. It's where I go in my head when this crap happens."

I was still worried. Brian said he'd talk to him, but I

didn't know if he had yet, and hard as it was, I decided to leave it alone.

Carol and Brian had talked me into staying. I wanted to go find John, but deep down inside, I knew they were right. I would be heading into the unknown, and God knew what else. It was an emotional decision that they had helped me see. My duty was here, here where I could do the most good. I'd have to worry about John, my oldest son stuck in Indianapolis, and his kids later. I'd have to trust John to do what was right and believe in his abilities to keep his kids safe. It was a different world since the EMP had taken out Washington, D.C. three months ago.

A few weeks after the battle, we'd convinced Rick, Sam, Gary, and Addison that it would be a good idea for all of us to live on one site. The problem was, we didn't have the room. The positive was, of course, we could better defend what we had.

With Allen and Sajan living in my cabin, we were crowded already. Adding four more people would be a struggle on a good day, and we had to make the move, plus get them all set up before the snow flew.

I knew we could make living space in my barn, plus that would be a good place for Sam's Ham Radio. The boys, Rick, Sajan, and Allen, could bunk in the barn. Rick, now an orphan, was Quint's grandson. Quint had been killed in the battle with the Looters. Sajan and Allen were friends of my youngest son Craig, they had walked from Appleton to my cabin and had quite a story to tell about their journey. We were building out a bunk room for them along with a small wood stove for heat. The main cabin was crowded to capacity, and even that wasn't ideal with Donna, my ex second-wife, and Craig sharing a room.

We had talked briefly about moving Craig into the barn with the other young men but hadn't decided yet. Addie, the young woman we had rescued from the Looter Gang, needed her own space, and we hadn't been prepared for that at all.

Sam is a retired Navy guy and avid HAM radio

supporter. It was his idea to build a cabin, actually two cabins, and that is what we would do. We could get a lot of materials from Quint's place. I still had a hard time calling it Rick's.

Rick agreed it would be a good use. In fact, we could get a lot of materials there. A cabin was decided on because it would be more solid, warmer in the winter without turning it into some overbuilt monstrosity like a house resembling the Taj Mahal.

The creak of the screen door took me from my thoughts as my son, Brian, my middle son, the active-duty Army Military Intelligence Officer, walked out the door, holding a steaming cup coffee, an AR strung over his shoulder.

Like me, he wore jeans and an OD T-shirt. His shirt was tucked in to his jeans, which were held up by a tactical leather belt that I know damn good and well he wasn't issued by the U.S. Army. He had always been a clothes horse, and I suspect he bought it online at warriorsareus.com or some such place before all the technology was fried. His jeans bloused over the tops of his boots, a habit I understood but was glad to be rid of after I retired from the army.

He plopped into the chair next to me, first unslinging the AR and resting it against the chair. It was astounding how quickly guns had become such a natural part of our everyday lives.

"Mornin," I said to him as he sat down.

"Uh, huh," Brian replied. "Who's on watch?"

"Always the officer, aren't you?"

"Just making sure, Dad. It's a habit."

"Sajan is out by the road, and Craig is in the back in the deer stand."

We had set up a deer stand in a tree near the garden, now filled with a little bit of everything. A potato mound was nearby—peas, beans, corn, tomatoes, zucchini, spinach, and lettuce. We also had carrots, radishes, onions, garlic, eggplant and a variety of other things. My little ten by ten garden plot had turned into several ten by twenty gardens that my grandson, Mike, was in charge of keeping the rabbits out of. He was good at it, too, as I had shown him how to set snares, and he had become a good shot with his .22. We ate a lot of rabbits.

"So what's on your mind this morning?" he asked.

"Same old stuff. All the things we have to do, the cabin, and how we are going to do that, working on some other things like a smokehouse and maybe a root cellar."

"We making a village?" he glanced sideways at me.

I shrugged. "Pretty much. Gonna need to eventually, might as well start now."

"Too bad we don't have feral hogs here," he quipped.

"We'll have to figure out how to get some pigs from someone. I'm sure we can trade. Maybe the Winstons," I said.

"Those are different people…" He left the sentence hanging.

"Yeah, but I like them. Honest, mean what they say, and you don't have to worry about them."

"I didn't say I didn't like them, just said they were different. So where are we gonna put the cabins?" He took a sip of his coffee and peered out at the land.

"I'm thinking either near the barn or the garden," Isaid.

"Gonna need an outhouse, Dad, the one we have isn't big enough."

"Shit hadn't thought of that."

We sat silently for a second and then started to laugh. It was nice to know that we could still laugh at bathroom jokes.

"What are you two laughing about?" a sleepy feminine voice came through the front screen door.

Brian and I saw Carol, my girlfriend of a few years, joining us after her Dinewr was burned down by roving looter gangs, standing there in grey athletic shorts and an oversized green t-shirt. Her disheveled brown hair, quite obviously, had not been brushed. Carol never stood much on those kinds of things, but I knew she hated the tangles from unbrushed hair.

"Guy stuff you wouldn't understand," Brian said with a chuckle as he casually took a sip of coffee, and avoided her gaze.

I noticed he was watching the door out of the corner of his eye. Obviously, Brian was smart enough to know that good situational awareness was a lifesaver after a crack like that to a physically strong, agile, and quick woman, even an Air Force woman.

"I'll show you some *guy stuff*, Brian, so don't start that garbage with me." She pushed open the door and padded on bare feet out onto the porch. She faked, raising a fist toward Brian, at least, I think it was a fake.

Carol padded over to where I was sitting, took the coffee out of my hand, turned, and sat in my lap. Sipping the hot drink, she paused and said, "Thank you, this is exactly what I needed."

"You know that's mine," I stated matter-of-factly, not thrilled with sharing, even with the woman I was falling in love with every day.

"Not anymore, I liberated it," she replied.

"I see where this is going. Get up," I said as I tried to stand.

A "grrrrr" came from her throat as she stood slowly to let me get out of the chair.

"Wash that out when you get done with it," I said as I walked down the steps.

"Don't go away mad, John," Carol shouted. "Just go away."

I wiggled all of my fingers, waving at her over my shoulder as I walked away. It was good to see everyone in a positive mood, but still, you don't mess with a man's first cup of coffee.

"Where're you going, Dad?" Brian said loudly.

"Out to the road to check on Sajan!"

If everything I had ever read was accurate, we were expecting or *should be* expecting the golden horde. It had been a few months since the grid went down. The first die-off of the sick, disabled, and overly dependent had happened. What was left was a mob of hungry people who most likely had robbed and taken everything available in the U.S. cities. They had formed gangs. It made sense that the next place they would look was rural. That's where all the farms were, that's where all the food was. Like the Mongol Golden Horde of the 13th and 14th Centuries, they would raid, pillage, take, and do what anyone desperate for food would do. We'd seen some refugees along the road, ushering most of them to keep going. A couple here and there had been invited to stay, move into one of the abandoned homes. Skilled people mostly, along with an EMT from Green Bay, who "had to get out of Dodge" as he'd put it. Brian said we had started our own immigration reform, and I suppose we had. Those we told to keep moving weren't thrilled, but it was hard to argue with a 5.56.

"Hello in the bunker," I announced as I came up behind it. I didn't want to startle anyone and get shot, so announcing myself seemed a good idea.

"That you, Mr. Henry?" Sajan's voice said from inside the log structure.

Sticking my head in through the door, I smiled and said, "Yep."

"Couldn't have been anyone else, I guess," Sajan replied somewhat sheepishly.

"Everything quiet?" I asked.

"Super quiet, Not even a deer crossing the road." Sajan was sitting on a log on the floor. His dirty khaki pants and long sleeve black shirt blended in well with the darkness of the inside of the bunker. We hadn't found him any boots yet. I made a mental note to ask Rahn if we could get boots for some of the young men. Far too many athletic shoes were being worn, and winter was coming.

"When's your shift over?" I asked.

"In about 2 hours or so."

"I'll take the rest of it. Go back to the barn and get a couple of extra hours of sleep. I'm gonna work you to death today, son."

He laughed. "You work us to death every day, Mr. Henry."

"Yeah, I guess I do that."

"Thanks, Mr. Henry. The belt is in the SAW, and a round is already chambered. I did a commo check over the phone about an hour ago with Craig. Everything is working fine."

We had patched all the phones together from the cabin to the two outposts so that we all could communicate with each other, in case of an attack.

"Who's my relief?" I asked.

"Donna."

"Go. Get some sleep, Sajan," I directed.

"Yes, sir," he said, grinning from ear to ear in that way only he could. An infectious mischievous one that, but still innocent amongst all of this tragedy and destruction.

I hunkered down in the bunker and started my vigil.

Chapter 2

"Courage is knowing what not to fear."

—Plato

The old DNR Fish Camp was starting to look like a fortress. Unlike Tom Harvey, Brad, the new leader of the remnants of the Looter Gang, had a sense of order and discipline about him. The main building he took as his place became a meeting hall for the leaders he had selected. The other buildings had been partitioned off with what they could scavenge or take from the homes and farms in the area. He only had the six men left from the raid on the "farmers," as he called them. Their group consisted of him and the six men, but there were also about fifteen women, and a few of them could be turned into fighters, especially the younger ones who had lost men in the fight.

Standing in the yard area in his filthy, oily jeans and heavy metal rock band T-shirt, Brad didn't look like much. The hatred inside was masked from all, except in his eyes. Few looked into those eyes without quickly casting away their own toward the ground. Brad ruled with an iron fist, and the whip he had fashioned with nails tied into it sent a clear signal that he would punish anyone without mercy.

His new number 2, Sid, was always close by. They both watched as a man ran toward them, a hunting rifle in his hand. As he got close, he stopped. "We got company, Boss. Some bikers at the gate."

"What do they want?" Brad asked.

"They want to see whoever is in charge."

"Well, that would be me," he replied with a chuckle. *Let's see what they want.*

Sid and the messenger man followed Brad as he strode toward the gate. As he approached, he saw three guys on motorcycles. The high bars behind their seats had weapons strapped to them, but the men were not noticeably carrying anything.

"Can I help you?" Brad shouted at the men.

"You in charge?" one of them asked. He was a big, burly man with a beard halfway down his chest. He wore a jean jacket, no shirt underneath it, adorned with a variety of patches and copious amounts of grease, oil, and dirt. His body was heavily tattooed.

"I'm in charge," Brad answered.

"Then, you and I need to talk," the man said.

"We can talk from here."

"I think we should talk privately," the man insisted. "How about we go over there?" He pointed toward a large maple tree about twenty yards away. "We can have us a conversation."

Brad stood there for a moment, thinking. *Why not?*

He nodded his head and walked toward the tree.

The man motioned to his two companions to stay put and took the same path toward Brad.

Brad turned to face the man. "So, what do you want?"

"We're taking over," the man announced calmly.

"The hell you are," Brad said, his voice filled with anger, his fists clenched at his side.

The biker glared at Brad. "Boy, don't bite off more than you can chew. We know you ain't but six or so men and a bunch of women. You can't stop us."

"No one is taking us over," Brad said again.

"One way or the other, we *are* taking over. With or without you." The threat was clear.

"We have the three of you outnumbered," Brad said. "You aren't taking over."

"Boy, just down that road, I have over thirty brothers

and sisters, all armed and none of them afraid to jerk a knot in your scrawny ass before we kill you. I'm trying to be polite here. We need each other, but not so much I can't put you in the dirt permanently."

Although his anger was raising, Brad stopped himself from saying something stupid. The man standing in front of him had every advantage. He had given Brad a chance to save face, but he needed time to think. Changing directions, Brad asked, "So, what's in it for me?"

"Now you're thinking, boy. What's in it for you? To begin with, you get to live."

"What's your name?" Brad asked him.

The man stared at Brad, skepticism, and curiosity in his eyes. "Roger, but they call me Rog."

"Rog?" Brad asked, lifting his eyebrows in question.

"That's what I said, kid. What do they call you?"

"Brad."

They stood there silently, each inspecting the other.

Finally, Rog spoke. "Kid, I'm not gonna stand around and measure dicks with you. We're taking over this camp and—"

"I need to save face," Brad said, cutting him off.

"Why?"

Brad shrugged. "I put these people together after a bunch of farmers shot us all to shit. I held us together, and I got us here. If you take us over, I look bad; I look weak."

"You *are* weak, kid, but I'll play. We'll call it a partnership for mutual benefit or some such garbage. I'm in charge, and you do what I say. In fact, you do what any of my guys say."

"What kind of partnership is that?"

"The kind that doesn't get you killed," Rog said bluntly. "Don't worry, kid. It won't hurt, and you'll learn to like it."

Brad put his hands in his pockets and stared at the ground. This hadn't gone the way he expected. He shuffled his feet in the dirt at the base of the tree, and raising his head, he said, "Okay, but let me tell my people."

"Sure. Go ahead, kid."

"Can you at least call me Brad?"

"Yeah, *Brad*," Rog said, dragging out the name with sarcasm. "You go tell your people. I'll be moving mine in today. That big center building will be fine for my top guys and me. You got that?"

"I thought we were partners?" Brad asked.

"We are. Some partners are more equal than others. Don't you read, kid? That's in *Animal Farm*. So you get moving, and we'll be back." Rog turned and walked toward the other two bikers.

"Let's go," Rog announced as he swung his leg over the seat of his motorcycle and started the engine. The other two mounted their motorcycles, and the three men rode up the hill, the loud mufflers of their bikes disturbing the otherwise peaceful countryside.

Brad strode back to his people standing along the gravel road.

"So what's up, Boss?" Sid asked.

Brad stood silent for a second, his hands clenching and unclenching into fists. Glaring at the dust on the road left from the motorcycles, he replied, "We have company for a while."

***

The Henry clan, as we were beginning to be called by our neighbors, gathered under the large tree by the garden where we had put the deer stand in order to watch the activity in the meadow.

"We're going to build a couple of cabins," I announced.

The looks I got in response ranged from believing I was crazy to curiosity.

"Why?" Carol asked. Her brown hair now hung below her shoulders and was held back by a piece of black ribbon she had found somewhere in the cabin. Her clothes were starting to hang a little loose on her, as were everyone else's. We were eating well, but our physical activity was beginning to show.

"We need to move Rick, Gary, Addie, and Sam over here," I said. "It's too hard with the few people we have to keep our resources secure and people safe."

"Rick's not going to like that," Donna chimed in. "That's his home, and his grandfather is buried over there."

"True," I replied. "He doesn't like it, but he's already agreed it's the right thing to do. It isn't going to be easy, but Sam and Gary have agreed as well. We can strip the house of materials to help make the cabins comfortable, like doors and windows. He'll have some of the house here."

"You aren't listening, John," Donna interrupted. "He's not going to like it. He might have agreed, but he will act out."

"I know, I know, but we don't have enough people to watch both places. We're going to have to come together on this issue. I don't know any other way."

Donna glared daggers. "Good luck."

A noise behind us caused everyone to turn and look. Nancy, Brians wife who had been wounded in our fight with the Looter Gang, was slowly making her way across the yard toward us. She was healing slowly but still had problems walking and speaking. Her head wound, healed on the outside, still caused her issues. Without better medical care, I had no idea how well she would fully recover.

"Hi, hon," Brian said. He went to her side and offered her to take his arm.

"No!" she said. "Let me."

And she continued on her path until she stood near us.

We were all glad to see that she was up, and while Grady, who thought he was a lap dog Great Dane, would occasionally get too excited when he was around her, almost knocking her over or sometimes causing her to stumble, yet she took it in stride. Grady was learning not to be so excited near her. Even so, sometimes she needed to support herself with a walking stick I had made for her. Nancy was still able to cook in the kitchen and cook she could do well.

She glanced at each of us now, silently asking what we were discussing.

"Dad wants to build cabins for the others, Rick and them," Brian said, filling her in.

Her eyes turned toward me, and she said, "Good luck."

"Yeah, I got that," I said, defeat in my voice.

"Let's move on. What kind of cabins are you thinking, John?" Carol asked.

"A dogtrot," I replied, grinning as I looked at King, Max, and Grady lying under a tree.

"What's a dog trot?" Donna asked, seeming to put her anger aside at last.

"It's basically two cabins connected in the middle with a porch that's open at both ends but covered by the same roof as the cabin.

"Interesting. I don't want to know how you learned of that design. How big does it need to be?" she asked.

I grinned. The woman had been married to me for some years. "I'm thinking two separate cabins about ten by ten with an eight-foot or so covered porch in the middle. Actually, two of them."

"Can we do that?" Carol asked.

I glanced Carol's way, meeting her eyes. "I think so. We have plenty of trees, and as I said, we can get other materials from Quint, I mean Rick's house. The hard part is going to be lifting the logs once the walls are above our shoulders, plus rafters for the roof."

"Sounds like a lot of logs, Dad," Brian interjected.

"I figure about forty-fifty for each cabin. Most of the logs will be ten feet long; a few will have to span the entire length of the cabin for stability."

"You have trees that big? Sounds like we need logs about fifty feet or so," Brian said.

I laughed. *Brian, always the skeptic.* "I do, plenty of them. Cutting them down is no problem; we have plenty of muscle power. Plus, there are huge stacks of logs already cut and trimmed on the far backside of the property. Actually, in the National Forest, but finders keepers. Paper companies cut them down and never came back. Getting them here will be a challenge, and then they have to be peeled and hewn. If we can get the portable mill working, that will help. Otherwise, we'll have to do it the old-fashioned way. With an ax."

"Whew. That's a lot of work, John," Carol said.

"Yeah, it is, but we have to do it. We have no choice."

"It's a good plan, Dad. When do we start?" Brian asked.

"Tomorrow is as good a day as any," I said.

"What about security?" Carol asked.

"Well, you ladies are going to have to take extra shifts. Everyone but Nancy, which isn't much. We still need to leave someone over at Rick's place to watch the road there, so we'll be short-handed for a bit."

"Too bad the First Sergeant isn't here," Brian added. "We could use the labor."

I nodded. "Agreed, but we can't ask or plan on that. Where's Mike?"

"He's out by the road with Craig," Brian said. "Those two are getting real close, and Mike spends a lot of time with him."

"That's good," Donna said.

"Mostly," he said grudgingly. "Except he's learning a few new words, and I'm looking for a bar of soap for both of them." Brian chuckled.

"Can't have little boys cussing. You never did," I replied, my eyes grinning at the fib.

"I still hate bar soap, Dad," Brian said.

"So, what's on the agenda today?" Carol asked.

"Gardening mostly," Donna answered Carol's question. "Plus, I need to inventory our canning supplies in case we need to go scavenging for more. A lot of what's in the garden is going to have to be put up and won't store in the basement well unless we can it."

"Time to work," Carol said. "Let's go."

I watched the group disperse, each to their own duties. Another long day was ahead of us.

Chapter 3

"Thinking about something long enough will not overcome the fear, but actions might."

—John Henry

He had been waiting over an hour to speak to the major. Rahn could see Wolfe every time the door opened. Standing inside the office, a folder in one hand and coffee in the other, Rahn decided that Wolfe was *intentionally* ignoring him.

Asshole.

It was almost another half-hour before the door opened, and whatever the meeting was about ended. Wolfe stalked out of the room and tried not to make eye contact with Rahn as he skirted around a couple of desks in the large open office area.

"Major!" Rahn said with a commanding tone.

Wolfe continued to ignore Rahn, so he spoke again. "Major? I need to see you, sir." The "sir" at the end of his sentence was borderline disrespectful, but it got the major's attention.

"What is it, First Sergeant? As you can see, I'm very busy," the major said.

"It's about the mission, Sir," Rahn replied, gaining control over his emotions and tone of his voice.

"What about the mission? It should be clear."

"Sir, have you seen the people across the road? How they are being herded about with summary punishments and confinement?"

"We are under martial law, First Sergeant. Those people violated any one of a dozen or more rules, some of them more than one."

"Those people, sir, are Americans. We shouldn't be treating them that way."

"In my office, First Sergeant. Now."

Once inside Major Wolfe's office, Rahn stood next to the doorway.

"Close the door, First Sergeant."

Rahn closed the door and stood silently, glaring at Wolfe.

"I don't like your tone, soldier."

"Sir, I don't like how we are treating our own citizens," Rahn explained his insubordinance. "That's just wrong. The people across the street at least have some semblance of decent treatment. Those across town are being treated like criminals."

"The order is lawful, First Sergeant," the major said. "Either get on board, or I'll replace you. It's that simple."

Rahn stood silent, thinking over Wolfe's ultimatum.

But before he could speak again, Wolfe continued. "The mission is simple. Round up those people out there and bring them into the camps where we can better take care of them. There are roving gangs and bands wreaking havoc, killing others, and whatnot. The decent people need our protection. Those people can be housed across the street. The resisters are considered criminals. If we bring them in, they go to Camp 2 or Camp 3. If they resist too much, you *end* the resistance."

Finding his voice, Rahn responded, "I agree we need to take *care* of them. We should be going after those bands, not rounding up decent people and putting them into what amounts to as a concentration camp. And what about the gun confiscations, sir?"

Slamming the folder on his desk with a loud slap, Wolfe stepped toward Rahn in anger. He seemed to catch himself and then, raising his voice, said, "Those are not concentration camps, First Sergeant.

FEMA has developed these camps to protect and provide for the American people. If they don't come in, they are criminals. We'll go after more criminals when we have safely secured the people."

Wolfe paused as if collecting his thoughts. "Those weapons are a danger to us all. We can't have them here in the refugee center, and we can't have people wandering around the countryside, taking potshots at each other. You will confiscate all the weapons you find. I have other teams going to homes and collecting weapons they find. Now you'll follow your orders, or I will replace you, do you understand?"

"Yes, SIR!"

"Now repeat your orders, First Sergeant. I don't want any misunderstanding or miscommunication excuses coming from you."

"Sir, I am to go out into the rural areas, gather up those people living on their own and in small bands. I am to transport as many as I can here while instructing those I can't transport to relocate here. I am to warn those who choose not to comply that they can and will be accused of not following the Martial Law Directive and that they will be treated as criminal elements. I will also confiscate any weapons I find, SIR!"

"And make sure that is what you do, First Sergeant. That includes your friends, the Henrys. Yes, I know you've become friends with them. We don't have time for friends, unfortunately, this situation is too grave."

Grave? What the hell is he talking about?

"I'm watching you, First Sergeant. We have a good thing here, and I'm going to be a part of this. Do your duty, follow your orders, and we can put this little chat behind us. Am I clear?"

"Crystal, Sir."

Rahn pivoted and walked out of the office. Tempted to slam the door, he thought better of it and headed for his Hummer.

***

CREEEEEEK, CRACK! The hemlock began to fall, crashing through the surrounding trees and rapidly moving toward the ground.

"TIMBERRR!" John shouted unnecessarily, and the tree thumped hard on the ground, sending a mild shock wave that everyone there felt. Branches continued to fall as the almost sixty-foot tall tree settled on the forest floor. The group waited a few minutes to make sure that no falling branches would hurt anyone, then went to work removing branches and cutting the tree into usable lengths of about twenty feet.

Brian brought up two harnessed horses dragging a skidding tong they had found in the barn of a neighboring farm. Attaching the tong to one of the logs, they dragged it out into a clearing and toward the meadow. It, along with all of the others, would find its way close to the barn. There it would be stripped of bark and hand-hewn into a log for a new cabin.

"The grounds are awfully soft, Dad," Brian shouted from the meadow. "The logs are still jamming into the dirt."

"Shorten the chain to get the leading edge up more. If that don't work, we'll have to make a skid of some kind. Like a sled for the log. I'll make sure Sajan and Rick do a better job of lopping off the branches, which will help."

"This should be the last load anyway," Brian replied.

"Yeah, I think we have enough. We'll have to get the portable sawmill from Rick's place," I said.

"I can ask one of the guys to go with me to get it, Dad."

A few hours later, all of the logs were lying near the barn. After having brought almost 50 logs the paper companies had cut down in the National Forest, there would be enough for the new building.

Craig and Allen were using draw knives to peel the bark off of the logs, most of which had been cut into twenty-foot lengths. Their bodies were glistening with sweat and covered with pieces of tiny bark and grime. Both boys, in spite of a sparser diet, had built muscle, and it showed. Piles of bark and wood shavings were gathered around their feet as they pulled the sharp knives against the logs, removing the bark. As they finished a log, it was rolled off of the heavy X-frames they had built to hold the logs, and another was muscled onto the frames for the next peeling. The freshly peeled logs were all moved to a stack waiting to be hewn into rough timbers for the cabin walls.

Brian stopped the team of horses. Behind them, trailed a string of logs that he had pulled from the other end of the meadow. "I have eight more for you!" he shouted.

Craig and Allen paused, wiping sweat from their faces.

"How many is that?" Craig asked.

"Should be about 40 or 50, not counting the others," Brian replied. "How many have you done?"

"About fifteen," Craig replied.

"I hope we have enough. How big is this cabin going to be?" Allen asked.

"Dad said two rooms of ten by ten for two cabins. I don't think we have enough," Craig said, his voice strained from tiredness. I'm guessing we are about halfway there.

"We'll be here all summer." Allen shook his head in despair.

"If they get that portable sawmill here, we can cut down on all this shaving."

"We got enough gas for it?" Allen asked.

"I hope so. There might be some in town at the old Quik Mart. Maybe we can siphon from the storage tanks again."

Across the meadow, walking with two horses came John, Brian, Sajan, and Rick. Brian was in the lead. They looked tired, but not half as tired as Craig and Allen felt.

As they got closer to the stack of logs, the sound of a vehicle coming up the drive caused everyone to stop and look. Craig and Allen grabbed their ARs, which were leaning against a nearby log. As they started to raise them toward the sound, they stopped. A U.S. Army HMMWV came into view.

"Looks like Rahn," Craig said.

***

The Hummer stopped and out stepped the First Sergeant. His ever-present driver, Specialist Johnson was getting out of the driver's seat. Another soldier stood in the turret, an M249 Squad Automatic Weapon mounted on a pedestal, his gloved hand resting on it.

Rahn saw John walking with two other men and three more men standing by logs and a pickup truck. Raising his arm, he waved, "Hello, Mr. Henry!"

"Is that how you greet a Warrant Officer, First Sergeant?" Brian replied with a laugh.

"Begging the Chief's pardon, sir, but I was speaking to your father," Rahn jovially replied with a flourishing hand salute.

Returning the salute out of custom as lifelong soldiers do, Brian replied, "What brings you our way, First Sergeant?"

"Let's wait for your dad; I don't like giving bad news more than once."

The men stood there, chatting as they waited for John to arrive. Brian was concerned about what the "bad" news was and tried to keep things positive as he and Rahn made small talk.

As John got within earshot, Rahn said, "Hello, Mr. Henry."

"Hello, First Sergeant," I said. "Thought I told you to call me John."

"Thought I told you to call me Chris," Rahn replied.

"No, you never said that Top," I replied. "I call bullshit."

"Well, it might be just Chris soon. We have a problem."

I looked at him. "Oh? How bad?"

"I've been told to bring you in."

"Bring me in *where*, and for what?" I asked.

"Major Wolfe said I have to bring you and everyone else here into the camp in Wausau."

"Well, that ain't happening." I rubbed my chin, trying to access what he was saying. "Nope. Not gonna happen."

"Oh, I figured that. If you saw those camps, you wouldn't want to go. We have three in Wausau now, and you'd be disgusted by the conditions," Rahn explained. "We're using GP larges with liners for shelter in some, turning schools into dormitories and athletic fields into compounds. They get an MRE bag a day to eat, plus a common breakfast, usually oatmeal and reconstituted eggs. And that's just for the good prisoners. The ones we have to force in get treated much more harshly."

"You're kidding, right? You're arresting people without cause, without a warrant?" Brian asked.

"Oh, it's worse. The people who are able to work are basically slave labor. They go out under guard, clean up the roads, find bodies and dispose of them. Those who refuse are put into a detention center, those who argue are put in a more secure detention center, those who object, you get the idea. It's all martial law, John."

"Geezus. Martial Law, my ass. Who declared that some tinpot dictator? The government from everything we know is gone. People are fighting out east over who's in charge. Troops in the Cheyenne Mountain are directing pockets of resistance or oppression. It's hard to tell from what we get on the Ham."

"It gets better," Rahn said. "Patrols like mine are going all over, rounding up more people. The excuse is, we have roving gangs raping, pillaging, and murdering. We tell them they need protection. For some, it's a good deal. Many others would be better on their own. The gang thing is legit. There have been a lot of murders, raids, rapes, and so on. You know all about that, though."

"We do, don't we, Dad," Brian said.

"All too well, son. So what's your plan, Chris, are you taking me in?"

"You know I won't do that. I can delay things for a while, but eventually, Wolfe is gonna make me act. I'll decide what I'll do then."

I glanced at the other soldiers with him. "How long do you think we have?"

"A little while. There are a lot of people between here and Wausau. But he did mention your group by name, so it won't be long."

We stood there silently, like most men not needing to say more. Rahn was visually inspecting our homestead. The large gardens, new privy, the work we'd done on the barn, and now all of the logs ready for use.

"What are the logs for? You building something?" he asked.

"Cabins. Decided it was time to move Rick, Sam, Gary, and Addie over here. Need the room before we do that."

"How'd the kid take it?"

I shrugged. "About as expected, but me, Sam, and Gary talked to him."

"What about the girl?"

"She's moving into my cabin to be closer to the other ladies. Craig is moving in the barn with Allen and Sajan."

"How long does it take to build a cabin?"

"With a good crew and all the right materials," Brian said, "a couple of days. For this group, maybe a week or two. Hardest part is heating the new buildings."

"That's right," I said. "I have one wood stove. I don't know if it'll be enough or if we need to build a fireplace. You feel like working up a sweat today?"

"No, I don't have time today. You could scavenge," Rahn suggested. "There have to be some in the abandoned homes."

"Could. We'll see."

Still sizing up the materials, Rahn asked, "Can you build two cabins?"

I laughed. "I'm already building two. You moving in?"

"You never know. I told you when I gave you all that stuff, I was hedging my bets. I still don't get warm fuzzies from Major Wolfe or FEMA."

"I thought Wolfe was a captain."

"He got promoted. He's the Officer in Charge up here now. So, can your family build two cabins?"

"Sounds like I'll need three. We'll see, First Sergeant."

"Chris."

"Yeah, Chris," I said. "Lots to do and not enough manpower. You know you and your boys therewould be welcome."

"I'll keep you updated, John. We probably need some kind of messaging system; the radios are being monitored."

"Sam said he expected as much. A lot of people talking in code or short bursts," Brian said.

"How about we use the old intersection over by Elmhurst, where 45 and 47 connect?" I asked. "We could put a rock pile off the road, put messages under it in a can, or something."

He nodded. "That'll work. If it's a hot emergency, I'll call Sam on the Ham."

"You sound like Dr. Seuss."

"There's a name I haven't heard in a while." Smirking, Rahn stuck out his hand. I grabbed it, and we shook. Then he shook Brian's hand. "Stay safe, Henrys," he said.

"You too, Chris," I replied.

He turned and climbed into the Hummer, twirling his index finger in the air signaling for Specialist Johnson to fire it up.

"Hey, Chris," I yelled before he could leave.

He pushed open his door and leaned his head out. "What?"

"Can you get us some footgear? Boots would be nice." I asked.

"Sure. What sizes?"

"Eight to Twelve, all regular."

"I can handle that."

I gave him a thumbs up.

As they drove out toward the highway, Craig strolled over. "So now what, Dad? What's next for us?"

"We're gonna need a lot more logs," John said.

Chapter 4

"Dressed in a Lions skin, the Ass spread terror far and wide."

—Jean De La Fontaine

The white farmhouse stood about 100 feet off of the road. The wide-open yard around it had a few outbuildings, and a UTV Mule was parked in the yard. A large garden plot was in an open field near the house, where stalks of corn, tomato plants, beans, and other vegetables were growing nicely that July. Across the road in front of the house, Brad sat and watched. He had been coming here for a few days, hiding behind an old bank building, and scouting out the group that occupied the farmhouse. The thick woods that bordered the bank was a perfect hide to observe the goings-on at the house across the street. What appeared to be several adults, a few children, and the one tbeing that concerned him the most— a dog—occupied the place.

A few vehicles had been pushed to the perimeter of the property, apparently as a barricade. No other visible defense was noticeable, although the group appeared armed with pistols.

As Brad watched, he couldn't help but laugh at the group. Their physical appearance was poor. Several of them seemed to need help moving around, and from the voices that he heard, a few never left the house. "Perfect," he said quietly to himself.

Ever since the bikers had taken charge, Brad found himself pushed into scouting roles more and more. Rog was obvious in his low opinion of Brad, but he didn't do much except ignore him or tell him what to do.

Brad didn't like it, and he certainly didn't care for how the bikers took all of the women for themselves, treating his six men like nothing more than slave laborers, keeping them away from the camp as much as possible. The bikers were pigs, food supplies were getting low, and Brad had to find more food somewhere. This little group of maybe ten people looked perfect for a raid. Brad thought he could raise his status if he could bring in a good haul. Now all he had to do was get back to camp, tell Rog what he had found, plan the attack, and take what was there. With this group at the farm, it would be as easy as taking candy from a baby.

***

Brad raced into the main building. Rog was in the corner with one of the women sitting in his lap, feeding him chicken. As Brad walked in, several of the bikers glared at him.

"What do you want, boy?" one of them asked.

"I need to see Rog," Brad replied, nervous but kept the resolve in his voice.

"What is it?" Rog asked.

"I found us a haul, a good one," Brad announced.

"Where is it? Bring it in here."

"We have to go get it. It's with a group."

"What do you mean, it's *with* a group?"

"A group of ten people. They look pathetic; we can take them easy," Brad explained.

"And…?"

"We need some men to go and take it."

"Go, then," Rog ordered. "Take your people and go get it."

"I need some of your men, too. I only have six; I need more than ten."

"So take six of mine. Shane, take some of the guys and go help this boy out."

"You got it, boss. C'mon boy, let's go figure out how we're going to do this. It better be easy, too, or you might not come back."

Brad stalked out of the building. Shane trailed, and behind him, four other guys followed.

"It should be easy, Shane," Brad said.

"If it's so easy, why do you need us?"

"Just being careful is all. My guys can probably do it, but I want to be sure. Plus, I think they have a lot of stuff. They have a UTV and a trailer; we'll need more guys to handle all that."

"You better be right, boy."

"I am." *I hope.*

***

"This is starting to look like a lumber mill," Gary said. The whine of the portable sawmill almost drowned out his voice. "Do we have enough yet?" he asked sarcastically.

"I hope so," I replied. "I'm tired of hauling logs out of the woods. We can start dismantling Rick's house after we get the dogtrot up. Then, we can finish it up while we start the other cabins."

"*Cabins*?" Gary asked. "I thought you were only building two."

"Three now. We have a lot of stuff to do, and before you know it, we'll be harvesting the garden and putting that up. Plus, I want to get the smokehouse up, too. Brian's going over to the Winstons to see if we can trade for a couple of pigs. I'd like a breeder and a few more. We can butcher and smoke some of the piglets, raise the others, and not have to eat game all the time."

"Plus, we'd have bacon," Gary said jovially.

I chuckled. "Don't start, man. You're gonna make us all hungry with that talk."

"I could go for a good steak, too," Gary said, smacking his lips at the memory.

Gary was watching the boys push logs through the mill. Most were just being squared up into timbers, the scrap getting put aside for firewood, or turned into boards. His now faded jeans and used-to-be-a-white t-shirt a dingy grey lending some character to both him and the scene around him.

"All in time, Gary. You jarheads are so impatient."

"Keep it up, doggie, keep it up," Gary said, using the Marine slang for a soldier. He wandered over a few feet and sat on a stack of timbers that had already been trimmed and stacked. Staring over at the foundation stones that had already been put in place with the first logs forming the sill plates already in place. "I'm getting old," he remarked.

"You and me both," I said, sitting next to him.

Rubbing my knee, I chuckled. "This new lifestyle is gonna do us all in eventually. Maybe the younger ones will adapt better. I thought I worked hard before; that was nothing compared to this."

"You solve the heating problem for these yet? I'm not looking forward to freezing my behind off this winter."

"Brian and Alan went out and found a few stoves in some of the abandoned houses. We need to take them out, along with all the stove pipe we can get. Even better, there are stacks of firewood at these places; it'll give us a good head start for winter."

"Excellent, my doggie friend, excellent. How long before these are done?" Gary asked, pointing his head toward the cabins.

"The dogtrot will be done in a few days, except for doors and windows. We need to get those from Rick's house. Probably another week to ten days for the other one. The biggest issue is shingles, believe it or not. I'm hoping we can recycle what's on the roof at Rick's. Otherwise, we're making shingles, and I really don't want to do that."

"I'm not even sure I know how," Gary said.

"Me, either. That's why I don't want to learn how to figure out how to do it. Besides, we'd probably need over a thousand wood shingles anyway. Not really feeling the mood."

"I hear ya brother, I hear ya," Gary replied. "I'm guessing you're going to put solar power in the cabin, at least for Sam's HAM radio?"

"Yeah, I can take one of the panels from the house and get power. I'm thinking we might want to look into making a generator from an old bicycle or something. I don't know of any solar panels in anyone's homes around here, and eventually, these are going to get damaged or just break. I've been lucky so far they survived the EMP."

"You know how to make one?"

"No, but I have binders as well as books and things stored on a USB drive, and we can always raid the library over in Antigo."

"Using those is a lot of work, John. It's not like we need the exercise." Gary and I almost simultaneously looked at our thinning bodies. "The younger folks all seemed to have slimmed, but some have gained muscle mass. I don't think we're going to be seeing a lot of fat people anytime soon."

"HEY! You, two old duffers, gonna gab or work?" Craig shouted from the log stacks.

"I guess we BS'd enough, Gary," I said as I stood. My knees creaked, and I grunted a bit from the effort.

Gary, his body, making the same music mine did, stood and headed toward his horse. Horses were becoming our preferred mode of transportation. We'd gathered a few from the area plus what Quint had.

"Too bad, I was enjoying the conversation." Taking the reins, he turned and said, "John, we need to start thinking about putting up hay and feed for the horses and other livestock. Not like we can run to the farm supply store anymore."

"Add it to the list, Gary," I responded as I waved my hand and walked toward the log stacks. *Just what I need, another manual exercise chore. But, its gotta be done.*

***

A lantern was visible in the window of the farmhouse. Its faint yellow glow stood like a beacon in the dark. Brad and Shane each had a group. Brad's group of six was behind the old bank across the road. His group would make the initial assault, striking hard and fast. The orders were simple. No survivors. They didn't need any women back at the camp, and they didn't need any children crying for their parents.

Shane's group had made its way around into the woods behind the farmhouse. They were there to stop anyone from escaping, and if needed, to go in as a second wave if Brad's group wasn't successful. Having spent half an hour behind the bank and in the woods next to it, Brad was convinced these people were fools, and this would be an easy grab.

I don't even know why we are here, except to take stuff back. All Shane had to do was wait. If the raid was successful, Brad would signal them to come in. If Brad wasn't successful, Shane would know and would attack in support. At least, that was the plan.

Rog had told him not to risk any of the guys. If Brad's little group was killed off, so be it. They had enough and could pick the farm off themselves later—after Brad weakened its defenders. If Brad was successful, the biker gang still came out ahead.

"It's a win-win," Rog said with a smirk.

Several hours had passed since the lantern was turned off in the farmhouse. The glowing cherry of a cigarette appeared on the porch.

They have a guard and cigarettes. Brad glanced toward the two men on his left and whispered, "Cross the road by the telephone pole over to your right where the road goes further back into the woods. When you get across the road, wait for my signal. I'll chuck a rock at you. Then, move up behind those buildings close to the house."

One man bent over and ran quietly across the road.

He ran so lightly his feet made no sound as he crossed the blacktop road. Brad followed them until he lost sight in the dark.

Brad waited a few more minutes before he threw a rock across the road. It thumped lightly as it landed in the distance.

"Shit, I hope he heard that," Brad said to himself.

A few minutes later, he saw them creeping up alongside one of the buildings in front of the house.

"Let's go, boys," Brad whispered to the others, and they moved aggressively across the road.

Entering the dirt and gravel drive, Brad raced up toward the front porch. The guard was obviously asleep. Taking his 12-inch buck knife out of its scabbard, Brad raked it across the sleeping man's throat, listening to him gurgle as he fell out of the chair and onto the porch. The dog, obviously old and slow, started to rise from its sleep.

Using the butt of his shotgun as a club, Brad put the dog back to sleep.

Brad and his band of six killers now surrounded the porch. In a low voice, Brad gave his orders. "No survivors. There are women in there, no fuckin around either; same goes with the kids. No survivors. Now make it quick."

Five of the men entered the house as Brad stood outside. Reaching toward the body on the porch floor, he looked for the cigarettes the man may have had.

"Shit," he said. "Blood-soaked. Shoulda shot him instead." A single scream came from inside the house, followed by a series of gunshots. In less than 30 seconds, it was over.

The men shuffled back outside, gathering around Brad. Out of the dark behind the house, Shane and his men arrived, the hoop earring on Shanes's ear, catching what light there was from the moon.

"That didn't seem too hard, boy," Shane remarked.

"It went easier than I thought," Brad replied.

Shane gathered up his men and slung his weapon over his shoulder. "Looks like you got a lot of work to do, boy, hauling whatever is in that house back to the camp."

Waving his arm toward his men, Shane walked off, his men following.

"Aren't you going to help?" Brad shouted.

"Boy, the deal was we'd help you take them out if needed; you're still doing the hauling. I'll let Rog know you did good."

***

Things were starting to look up as we made progress on the cabins. As it turned out, hauling rock and cinder blocks we found was harder than the construction of the cabins themselves. All of the walls had been done and much of the roof on both. Finding pallets of shingles, even though they didn't match, was a godsend. You take what you can get in an apocalypse.

It was mid-day, and work was progressing well. Gary and I were standing side by side, inspecting our handy work of leading everyone else in building the cabins. It wasn't that we didn't help; we did help raise logs on the walls and put up the purlin logs to help support the roof and keep the walls together.

Craig came toward us, having just come down from the roof of one of the cabins. Surprisingly, he didn't look tired, just sweaty and dirty.

"Dad," he shouted and raised his arm toward me.

I thought he was waving, and then he shouted again. "Dad!"

The pointing was obvious. Turning around, I saw Donna walking toward us, a young woman, and two young kids with her.

"Son of a bitch," I said angrily under my breath.

The young woman was dirty and looked tired. Her long brown hair was held in a ponytail with what looked like a ribbon of dark cloth. She wore camouflaged woodland pants, tan desert boots, and a tan t-shirt. Over that, she had a dark, unzipped hoodie.

The two blonde kids with her—I assumed they were hers—dragged themselves along, the oldest couldn't have been more than five or six.

"John, just shut up and listen," Donna said as she led the woman and her kids toward us.

"You know the rules, Donna," I replied.

"I said, shut up and listen."

I stared at the kids. "Okay, explain."

"I was out front on guard and saw her. Her name is Linda, by the way, coming down the road. They looked tired and thirsty, so as we agreed, and you did agree with that, John, so I took her and the kids some water."

"So, why are they back here?" I asked.

The woman, Linda, was glaring at me with a shut up-before-I-kick-your-ass look.

"She has pharmacy training, John. We need those skills."

"I can hunt, gut a deer, garden, and do just about anything else, too," Linda explained from behind Donna. "I grew up on a farm, Mr. Henry. I know how to do things." My boys and I were run out of our place near Chilton. We need a place to rest."

"So why'd you come all the way here?" I asked. "That's 150 miles away."

"I have family in Antigo. Well, I hope I still have family in Antigo," she replied. "We were trying to get there." She stepped toward me; there was no give in this girl. "I don't even know if they're alive, Mr. Henry. My boys and I need a place, and I'll work for it."

I looked over the young woman's shoulder back at Donna; actually, I glared at her. "We have rules, Donna, and we can't take everyone in." Then I turned and walked away.

After a few steps, I stopped, turned, and looked at the young woman. "My name is not Mr. Henry. It's John." Then, I headed back to where the cabins were being built.

"What does that mean?" Linda asked Donna.

"It means you get to stay."

Linda almost leaped forward as she hugged Donna. "Thank you," she said.

"Let's get you and these kids back to the cabin, cleaned up, and fed," Donna said. "We have a lot to do."

As the two women and boys headed toward the cabin, Linda asked, "He's kind of an ornery cuss, isn't he?"

"You have no idea," Donna replied. "You have no idea."

***

The long day had ended. It was quiet on the porch, and I enjoyed the quiet. I was sitting in my usual spot, a cigar in hand, with about two fingers of whiskey in a glass, neat. I missed ice. We didn't have any and I would have to, among a thousand other things, think about building an icehouse. Then, we'd also have to think about how to get the ice to the icehouse and from where. The challenges never ended.

The creak of the screen door told me I was about to have my peace interrupted. The shroud of darkness made it hard to see, but the shape and its height told me who it was.

"You like some company?" Carol asked.

"Sure," I said, patting the arm of the wooden chair next to mine. The two chairs had been placed that way shortly after I moved into the cabin permanently. Of course, then I wasn't seeing Carol. We'd just chat when I was at her diner. Over the years, we got closer, and she started coming out to the cabin for the day, then the night, and sometimes for longer than a night. Now she lived here.

She was wearing cut off denim shorts and one of my OD t-shirts. She came over and sat down, waving her hand rapidly in front of her face. "Blow your cigar smoke in the other direction, John," she said with a chuckle.

"Yes, Ma'am," I replied and quickly blew a big cloud in front of me. "Keeps the skeeters away," I said with a fake hillbilly accent.

"It's getting crowded here," she said. "Are you sure we don't need more cabins?"

I chuckled. "Why, you want your own? I thought you enjoyed snuggling up with me at night."

"I wasn't suggesting getting my own place, John Henry. If I need one of those, I still have my house in town. I thought if we get any more people here, we'll need more room. Don't worry; I'm not leaving you."

"I guess I should learn how to tease better. I didn't mean anything by it."

"If you can't take it, don't dish it out is what my commanding officer always said," she replied, punching me lightly on the arm.

Our hands found each other, and we sat there holding hands and whispering in the dark. For a short while, it seemed as if we were in the before the EMP hit time, and it was a nice feeling.

"I'm glad you're here, Carol."

"Where else would I be?" she asked.

I detected sarcasm. "You know what I mean. I'm glad you're here, with me, us together."

"I'm glad I'm here too, John. I'm not leaving. I'm here for the duration."

Chapter 5

"Direct threats require decisive action."

—Dick Cheney

It took two days for Brad and his group to move the food, weapons, ammunition, and other supplies from the farmhouse. They hadn't even touched the barn or outbuildings but knew they had a cache that would help beyond their dreams or imagination.

Sitting on the ground leaning against the UTV tire, Brad wiped the sweat from his forehead and let out a sigh of exhaustion. He was tired. The summer heat was building toward the warm days of late July and August. Without the benefit of electricity for air conditioners or fans, or even for cold drinks, the summer was going to be rough. The crunching of footsteps across the dirt caused Brad to raise his head. Squinting into the sun, he saw a figure that he immediately knew coming closer.

"Hello, Rog," Brad said.

"You did good, kid. This is quite the haul," Rog said.

"Thanks. I told you I'd found a good one."

"Yep, that you did." Rog turned to walk away.

"Rog…" Brad almost shouted.

Rog turned back and stared at him.

"You said we were a team," Brad said. "You said you'd help me with the farmers. I delivered, now it's your turn."

"You've got balls, kid, I'll give you that," Rog said with a chuckle.

"You said you'd help," Brad insisted.

"Okay, kid, I'll help. Tell me what your idea of help is."

Brad shared what he knew about the farmers. The farmhouse where the battle took place, how well-armed the farmers were, and that he thought there had to be another house or farm nearby. He just didn't know where.

"Okay, so you know shit, and you don't know shit. What's in it for me?" Rog said. "What do you want me to do, and what in the fuck do *you* want to do?"

Brad's expression turned dark as a mask of anger wrapped around his eyes. "I want them dead. I want them all dead except that little girl, the one that escaped. I want her for something special."

"Geezus kid, a bit pissed at them, aren't you?" Rog said. His head fell back as he laughed harder. Putting his hands on his thighs, he leaned forward, inches from Brad's face. "Now, what's your plan, kid?"

***

Two of the cabins were now finished. We had removed all of the doors and windows from Quint's place—*damn I missed that cranky old man*—putting all that we had not used inside the barn.

Sajan and Allen had laid the foundation for the third cabin. All three would be in line; it was starting to look like Boonesborough, the frontier settlement of Daniel Boone way back in the 1700's; all we needed was a log fort to go around it.

Craig and I had built a smokehouse. I really needed to find some pigs. The deer population, even with all of our activity hauling logs and patrolling appeared to be growing. Venison would be plentiful as would turkey this fall.

Mike was still bringing in rabbits, and he had gotten very good at skinning and gutting them. He sometimes had to wrestle with Grady, Max, and King over a rabbit carcass, but it all worked out in the end.

One day, I saw Nancy watching him do that, the two new boys, Caleb and Ethan, hovering over him as if he was their newfound leader. The two boys followed him around everywhere, and Mike was eating it up.

I spoke with Nancy about it. She was sad that her son had become such a country boy and "so outdoorsy" as she put it.

"Does it really bother you?" I asked.

"Yes and no, FIL," she said, using the nickname she had given me "My little boy has grown up so fast, but I know that if he doesn't, he may not grow up anywhere."

I could sense the emotion in that statement and the stark acceptance of our new reality. We had to survive or perish. That was our choice. We were all doing it with a bit of a twist, though, as we seemed to be on the verge of thriving. All we needed was more meat options.

We'd got Sam's HAM radio set up in the new cabin. He was tapping away at his keys and talking to people all over the country. Sometimes, he got what he called a "skip," and we could listen in to foreign transmissions, mostly from France and Germany. If we were lucky we'd get London, or what we thought was London. All in all, things were not going well all over the world. Between rogue bands that had become small armies to equally rogue FEMA that were basically the same thing, things had turned to shit. What surprised me the most was the powerhouse that FEMA had become. They were not necessarily the helpful, benevolent group that we had come to think they were established for. A large number of FEMA associates had set up camps and turned them into slave labor.

Sam found out a lot of resistance groups had formed. Sam, Gary, and I, during one of our evening chats, decided that the world had returned to living like people had in the past—medieval times, only with guns. We knew that one day the guns would be mostly useless, and at best, we'd be back to flintlock muskets and swords. We'd have to find some, learn to make some, and then figure out how to make black powder from scratch.

Gary said he could make a crossbow and be like that guy in the zombie TV show. Our laughter at him was not kind, but he'd laughed, too.

The new girl, Linda, was pulling her weight, what little there was of it. A skinny brunette, she had a lot of bark. She and Donna were doing wonders finding native medicinal herbs, maintaining the herb garden that Donna had started, and creating concoctions for everything from headaches to sniffles to my back pain.

I didn't hear Brian walk up behind me as I was deep in thought about all we had done and all we still needed to do.

"Dad," he said.

I jumped. "Jesus Christ, Brian, don't sneak up on me like that."

"I didn't sneak, Dad. I walked up behind you."

"Bull shit," I said with a grin. "You snuck up on me."

"We have to go out to the bunker. Carol has a problem she needs you to see."

"What kind of a problem?" I asked.

"Bikers."

***

"Are you fucking nuts, kid?" Rog shouted. "I'm not sending my guys over there on a wild goose chase attack."

"How about you send them out as scouts? Cruise around and see if they find anything?" Brad asked.

"That's good thinking, kid, but gas is getting low."

"There's two 500 gallon gas tanks at that farmhouse. Both seem to be full."

"And just *when* were you gonna tell me about that? You holding out on me?" Rog reached down and grabbed Brad by the collar of his t-shirt, jerking him to his feet. "You holding out on me, kid?" Rog said through clenched teeth.

"N-n-no," Brad replied. "We hadn't figured out how to get it here yet."

"I saw gas cans in one of the buildings here; the 5-gallon jerry can style. I bet they have some at that farmhouse, too."

"Okay, we'll use them. So go get the gas, bring it back here. We'll fill up the bikes, and I'll send Shane out with a couple of guys, and you can do some scouting."

"I don't know how to ride a bike," Brad said, his voice barely above a whisper.

"Didn't say I'd give you one. You'll ride bitch behind one of the guys."

***

Brian and I walked toward the Bunker. As we approached it, he stopped, putting his closed fist into the air, his arm in the shape of an "L."

"What are you doing?" I asked.

"Hand signs, Dad," he said, giving me one of his infectious grins. "This means halt."

"I know what it means, dumbass. Why are you doing it?"

"You'll see. We need to get low and move up to the bunker."

We both d.ropped to our knees and did a low crawl toward the bunker. Well, I did a hands and knees crawl to the bunker. I had no intention of snaking on my belly through the woods unless someone was shooting at me.

We crawled into the bunker. Carol was there, looking down the road through a pair of binoculars. In a low voice, I asked her, "What's up?"

Taking the binoculars away from her eyes, she looked at me. "Bikers, they've been up and down the road all day."

"Are they traveling through?" I asked.

"No, it's the same ones. I think they went down to Quint's place."

"How many?" Brian asked.

"Three bikes and four riders. One bike was doubled up."

"How long have they been here?"

"All day," Carol replied.

"Craig says he's seen 'em around before. They've driven by, sat in the middle of the road up on the hill, just watching," Brian said.

"And I'm just now hearing about this why?" I asked. If there was a threat, I needed to know about it right away.

"Everybody who's come to the bunker has been told to watch for them, Dad. We've got it covered."

"I felt when they started nosing around the drive to Quint's place it was a good idea to tell you," Carol interjected. "They weren't just joy riding anymore."

"Well, at least somebody's thinking," I remarked. I crawled out of the bunker and through the woods toward the cabin. As far back as we were, I knew they couldn't see us, but they could have heard us. The cabin building and other work was noisey. Unless their bikes made them almost deaf, they had to have heard us working. I had to find Craig.

It didn't take long. He was by the hand pump flirting with Addison. The two of them had become close, and I caught them kissing the other night.

While on the one hand, I was happy for them both, the last thing we needed was romance around here. Romance led to other issues we weren't equipped to handle.

"Craig!" I shouted. "Quit flirting with Addie. I need to talk to you."

I had startled Addie clearly, as she jumped, and then, lowering her head, she scurried past me, muttering, "Hello, Mr. Henry."

"I told you it was John," I replied, as she went past.

"Dad," Craig said, the frustration obvious in his voice. "We were just talking."

"You were flirting. I'm not blind," I answered. "Now, tell me about the bikers."

"Sure. Those fuckers have been cruising up and down the road for the last few days. I'm surprised you didn't hear them."

"I musta gone deaf in my old age. I didn't hear them, and you shoulda told me."

"I told Brian. He said he had it covered. You can't do all this alone, Dad."

I stared at him, the wheels in both of our heads turning. He was right, and he knew that I knew he was right. I *couldn't* do this alone. Hell, I didn't want to do *any* of this at all, but here I was. We now had 15 people in the homestead. Plus, the Winstons and a few families still scattered about on some of the farms nearby, not to mention a couple of houses in town.

There was the Rez, but I hadn't been over there in years. Far too many had pulled out, some going to Wausau and others just plain leaving. There was no way I could be responsible for all of them.

"You're right, son. I can't do it alone, and I need all of you to help. You've been doing that."

He nodded an affirmative. "Yes, we have, Dad."

"We need to talk about this tonight after dinner. Except for whoever is on guard in the bunker and back, we need to gather on the porch and talk it over," I said. "Who's on guard tonight, do you know?"

"Donna's in the back and Allen's by the road."

"I'm impressed. I didn't even know that there'd been another switch." A bit of pride came through in my voice knowing my youngest son was stepping up.

"After dinner, we'll meet on the porch. I want you to tell everyone what you saw, and I'll have anyone else who saw anything do the same. Then, we'll sort it out and figure out what to do. The bikers have to know we're here. And we need to be prepared for their response."

***

"Shane!" Rog shouted across the camp.

Shane had just returned with the other 2 bikers and was stretching his back after the long ride. Glancing toward Rog, he waved and started to walk toward him.

Rog waited for him while eating a sandwich. *Good thing someone here can bake bread.*

"What's up, Rog?" Shane asked, eyeing the food in Rog's hand.

"What'd you find out? Have you found Brad's farmers?"

"Yeah. They're close to that farmhouse where Brad got his ass kicked. The house has just about been taken apart. Doors and windows are gone, boards taken off the porches, the roof is missing, and no one is there."

"How close?"

Shane cocked his head to the side, remembering. "Not far, there's a path through the woods in the back of the house that looks well used. I think I saw a road heading into the woods not far from this farmhouse. Jake says he thought he heard hammering and machinery, too."

"Who the hell has machinery nowadays?"

"It's what he said he heard, Rog. I believe there could be hammering. Not so sure about the machinery, though."

"You guys keep going over there and watching. Don't start any shit, just watch."

"No problem, Rog. We can do that."

***

I found Carol just where Craig had said she'd be. "Let's get the UTV and take a ride."

"You mean, like a date?" she asked coyly.

"Ha! No, I want to go into town and check things out."

"Why not use your truck?"

I shook my head. "They're using it to haul things from Quint's and the barn for the cabins."

We were both already armed. We hopped onto the

UTV, I gave it some gas, and we shot off down the driveway and out toward the road, turning toward town.

We passed a few stragglers along the way. They didn't even look at us as we whizzed by. I refused to call them Walkers, which is what Craig had named them. His sense of humor was getting annoying. Yet, I understood it, too. If we didn't make light of the situation, then it would gnaw at us, and that wasn't good, either. It is similar to the dark humor soldiers at war use; you do what it takes to survive.

We cruised past the burnt remains of the Quik Mart, and not too far down the road the pile of burnt wood and debris that had been Carol's Diner. I started to accelerate, but Carol put her hand on my arm.

"It's okay, John. I'm over it now."

It was then that I saw them. Three bikers on the road in front of me, just sitting there on their bikes staring at us. I stopped the UTV and said, "Be ready, Carol, that may be them."

"When I saw them, one was riding double, but it could be them," she said.

One of them reached behind himself and pulled out an AR, then aimed it at us.

"Look out, Carol," I shouted and pushed her down in the seat. I heard a roar, and lifting my head up, saw them riding away. I don't know if that was a warning or not, but *no one* points a weapon at me or my family.

"You alright?" I asked her.

"Yeah, I'm fine. What happened?"

"One of them pulled out a weapon and aimed it at us." Pausing, I added, "This is why I should have been told about this."

"What, your knowing would have prevented him from pointing a gun at us? Geezus, John, you can't control everything, and you can't do this alone. Dammit, you frustrate me sometimes."

"Uh huh," I muttered.

Turning the UTV around, I headed back to the cabin. "We'll talk about it later," I said.

I knew she was right, but I still felt I had to be the protector. I had to do this. But she was right. I needed every damn one of them, and that was my problem. Somebody or more than somebody was going to die, and I didn't want it to be any one of the people who had become my family.

***

Supper was the now normal cacophony of noise and distraction. Three kids, twelve adults, and three dogs make a lot of noise, most of it unintelligible. We had to figure out what we were going to do come winter because I didn't think it was a good idea to have individual meals for the cabins or boys in the barn. Once the snow started flying, just a few months from now, and the temperature dropped, it would be more efficient to have a large single meal for everyone. That probably meant doing some modifying in the main cabin.

Between three boisterous young boys, four young men, a comedian, four women, and three old guys, we managed to get everybody fed. Nancy was doing a killer job managing both our food and the kitchen, and we did so without any fights, complaints, or tears. I loved the look on Craig, Rick, and Sajan's faces when Nancy told them they had clean up.

I told everyone that once the clean up was finished, we would meet on the porch and talk about things. I, of course, wasn't cleaning anything.

Brian and I went outside and set up a few chairs on the porch. He started to move mine, and I had to let him know, firmly, that my chair wasn't moving. It had been in that place for several years and was going to stay there till I died. He could move it afterward.

The evening was beginning to settle in as everyone began to troop out onto the porch. Donna and Allen were on guard duty. I'd talk with them later and bring them up to date.

I sat in my chair, craving a cigar. I didn't have many left that people knew about, though I did have a good stash hidden in the basement. So, for now, the craving would simply have to pass until the meeting was over.

Nancy and Linda had hot tea. I had plenty of teabags, and Donna had already shared she could start collecting plants and herbs from the garden for making tea once the commercial stuff ran out. I was rather impressed at all of the skills we had learned without seeming to try. We were so fortunate.

The kids were sitting near their mothers. Craig, Addie, and Sajan were on the steps, and Gary, Sam, and Rick were sitting on a bench against the wall of the outside of the cabin. Brian was in the chair across from me, and Donna sat in a chair next to Nancy and Linda.

"I'm glad everyone could make it," I started.

The laughter I expected from my joke didn't happen. "We have some things to talk about that are important for everyone to know." I looked at each of my people, my newfound family, to make sure they were all paying attention. I wasn't trying to be dramatic or scare anyone, but I needed them to understand the seriousness of the situation.

So like a coward, I began with things less serious.

"We've got two of the cabins finished," I said. "We can move some of the furniture from Quint's place, important things like beds, chairs, and so forth. We've dug a privy."

I could tell by the looks on a few faces they either didn't like that idea or didn't know what a privy was.

"We have to start using it. So, once everyone moves into the new cabins that's going to move into them, the bathroom in the house will get a much-needed break. Sam, Gary, and Rick can move into one cabin half. Linda, Caleb, and Ethan will go into the other half. Craig, Sajan and Allen will move into half of the second cabin and Addie will get the other half."

I stared hard at Craig. "Don't make me regret that."

I think I embarrassed him but I didn't care.

"Nancy, Brian, and Mike will keep their one bedroom in the cabin. Carol and I will share my bedroom, and Donna will keep the one she and Craig have been sharing. If anyone is unhappy with these arrangements, work it out between yourselves. I have no problem with people trading and switching around."

As I looked around the group, I didn't see any objections or hurt feelings, which was good. I did notice a sidelong glance between Craig and Addie.

"We need someone to go to the Winstons. No one goes alone, so it will have to be two someones, to see if we can trade for some pigs. Gary, if you don't mind, I'd like you to go."

Gary nodded. "I can do that, John. I'll take Rick with me. He knows the Winstons pretty good."

"Sounds like a plan. You okay with that, Rick?" I asked.

Rick sat up taller. "Yes, Mr. Hen— I mean, yes, John."

I smiled at him. The kid was trying. He wanted so much to fit in. We were all he had now, and making him feel important gave him confidence.

"We have to finish the third cabin. That's next on the list of to do's. If Rahn ends up joining us, my guess is he'll bring Specialist Johnson and a few others along with him. We'll need the space. No one needs to spend the winter in the barn. It's bad enough that's where we have to put Sam's HAM radio setup." I looked around, making eye contact with every person there. "I'd also like for us to give some thought to building a greenhouse using some of the extra windows from Quints's house. If we need more, we can take them from abandoned houses. Our garden is a good size, but we'll have to expand it next year. We'll need the greenhouse to grow fruits and veggies to get us through the winter. Linda, can you manage that project? You said you grew up on a farm."

"Yes, sir, Mr. Henry," she replied. "The boys will help me."

I thought Craig and Brian were going to burst when she said "sir" they were trying so hard not to laugh.

I winked at her. "I told you before my name is John. Mr. Henry was my dad or is this bonehead sitting next to me." I gestured towards Brian with my head.

Linda smiled, but nodded her head up and down. I knew she was going to call me Mr. Henry again. She had that sassy look about her that said she would.

"Okay, the main reason I wanted everybody here tonight was to talk about a growing problem that affects us all. Our safety is at risk, and we need to figure out what we are going to do about it."

"Are you talking about the bikers, John?" Sam asked.

"Bikers?" Mike quickly asked.

"Yes, Mike, bikers," I answered my grandson, pursing my lips together.

"Uncle Craig calls them the fuckers, isn't that right, Uncle Craig?" Mike said, glancing at Craig.

I thought Donna was going to turn purple.

I saw Brian out of the corner of my eye place his hand over Mike's mouth, and Mike suddenly found something interesting on the floor of the porch. Another hand grabbed Mike by the back of his shirt.

"Young man, you do not EVER use that word, do you understand me, Michael Henry," Nancy said.

"Yes, Mom," Mike said, his voice breaking.

"And YOU Craig Henry, you should be ashamed," Nancy continued her rant. "This boy worships you. Don't you be teaching him any bad habits. Lord knows he's learning enough as it is."

I couldn't tell if Craig was scared or embarrassed. What I could tell is he was shocked. As I was wondering exactly what he was feeling, a very small and contrite voice said, "Yes, Ma'am."

An awkward silence weighed heavily over the group. Downcast eyes, upcast eyes, and shared looks of "uh-oh."

Taking a deep breath, and then another, I said, "Okay, everyone. Can we please stay on task here."

I let my eyes trace around the porch, again making eye contact with everyone.

"So back to the bikers," Brian smirked.

"Knock it off, Brian," I said.

"Sorry," he answered, and then suddenly jumped off the porch and ran behind the cabin. It didn't take long before we could hear him laughing.

"Anybody else?" I asked. When no one moved, I said, "Okay, then. Carol and I ran into three bikers this morning not too far from her diner. They were sitting on their bikes in the middle of the road, and one of them shot a weapon at us."

"Is he dead, Dad?" Craig asked.

I just looked at him, that look a father gives to his son when the question he's asked is so ridiculous and doesn't need to be answered. "These bikers are looking for trouble. I'm convinced they were searching for us. Linda, do you know anything about these guys?"

She shook her head. "No, Mr.—John. I don't. I get why you ask, me being new here. I don't know them and haven't had anything to do with them." She reached down and put her hands on her two boys, who sat at her feet.

Brian came back up on the porch and slid down into his chair. "Sorry," he said.

It sounded sincere, so I let it go.

"We need to stay vigilant," I said. "No contact with them. If you see any of these bikers, let others know. When Gary and Rick go to the Winstons, they can ask if they know anything else. These guys do *not* come onto this property. Avoid conflict at all costs, but if they attempt to drive up on the property, rules of engagement are to shoot them on sight. Any questions?"

No one said a word. They knew I was serious.

The shuffling of feet, combined with a few squirming behinds in chairs, told me it was time to end the meeting.

"Okay, we're done here. Everyone can go about their business. Craig, Brian, I need to speak with you two."

"Yes, sir," they both replied.

Sometimes to set the tone, it's important to not

correct how they answered me. I needed their help with a plan of action.

Chapter 6

"Experiencing the pain of loss can be a motivating force."

—John Henry

The noise inside the cabin told me my morning quiet time on the porch was coming to an end. People were starting to stir, and I could hear someone in the kitchen banging away at things. Quiet time interrupted, Gary and Rick stopped by to let me know they were heading to the Winstons.

Max and King, in their usual spots on the porch, were snoring. Grady hadn't come down, but as soon as Mike was up, he'd be here, too. The stirrings indoors obviously not concerning enough to awaken either of my dogs.

A creak of the screen door got their attention as Carol came out. Her mussed hair splayed all over highlighted the sleepy smile she sent my way. She jumped as Grady pushed open the door, nudged her aside, and went to lay down beside Max and King.

Mike must be awake.

"Mornin," she said with a still sleepy voice. "How is it you always manage to get up so early?"

"Old habit, I guess," I said. "Never could sleep in. Well, at least since after I joined the army. Even if I go to bed late, I wake up before the sun. I learned to like the morning."

"Hmmph," she replied as she grabbed my coffee cup. It was empty.

"You drank it all?" she said, pouting.

"I've been out here a while. Want some?"

"Yeah, but I'll get it."

"Okay."

She gave me *the look.*

"What?" I asked.

"You were supposed to argue and say you'd get me some anyway."

I grumped a look back at her. "Then you'd steal my chair."

"Men," she exclaimed and went back inside.

It wasn't long before I heard more pots and pans banging in the kitchen. It sounded like Carol was doing more than making coffee, which had already been made in the pot on the stove.

Max, Grady, and King were now fully awake and sitting up. "I suppose you guys want breakfast," I said and stood up from my chair. They didn't move.

I walked into the kitchen, heading toward the pantry where the dog food was. "Gonna feed the dogs," I said loudly as Carol heated up a frying pan. "Thought you wanted coffee?"

"I do, but I'm hungry. I thought I'd make breakfast and then take a trip over to my place. I have some seeds and a few other things I want to get. It'll be a nice diversion."

"Are you sure that's wise after yesterday? Want me to go with you, hon?"

"Hon?" She lifted an eyebrow, clearly still mad. "I'll be fine. I'll take one of the boys. They're getting restless with all work and nothing else. Be good to get away."

"Be safe. Keep an eye out for those bikers. You may see Gary and Rick, too. They headed out to the Winstons' early and will have to go by your place on the way back."

"Okay," she said as she added sausage links to the frying pan.

She was still upset with me. "You alright?"

"I'm fine, John. I'm just tired, and there is never any time to just sit back and relax."

"You could get up early with me and sit on the porch." I got the look again. "Why, I've gotten used to sleeping a little later since I moved in with you." Carol said.

The smell of venison sausage had apparently woke up Mike as he padded downstairs and into the kitchen.

"Mornin' Mike," Carol said, giving him a big grin.

"Mornin' Miss Carol," he answered. "Are you making venison sausage?"

"Yep, want some?"

"Uh-huh… I'm starved," he said.

"Don't I get any?" I asked.

Carol rolled her eyes at me. "Maybe," she replied.

We ate our breakfast, I did get sausage, and while we were finishing up, Brian and Nancy came into the kitchen, followed by Donna and Linda.

"We smelled breakfast," Donna announced.

Behind her came Linda's two boys, Caleb and Ethan.

"Hi Mike," Caleb said.

"Hi," Mike replied.

"Nancy, would you mind if Mike went with me to my old place today?" Carol asked. "He's been a big help to me making breakfast, and I'd like to give him a bit of reward."

Nancy put her fork down and looked at Carol. "Gee, Carol, I don't know. After you ran into those bikers yesterday, it seems a bit dangerous."

"I wanna go, I wanna go!" Mike chanted. "Please, Mom. Please?"

"I'm taking Allen with me, too," Carol added. "We will be okay."

"Allen is pretty responsible. I'm not thrilled with it, but I suppose. Mike, you better listen to her. I mean it!" Nancy said, giving Mike her strict Mom's look.

"Yaaa! Thank you, Mom. I will, I will." With that, he dashed out of the kitchen and headed upstairs.

"I'm going to go ask Allen. He doesn't know yet," Carol remarked with a quiet chuckle.

"You taking horses, the UTV, what?" I asked.

"If it's okay, can we use the UTV?" Carol asked sweetly.

"Yeah, we're still good on gas. I'll need to make a trip to the old gas station soon and siphon out enough to fill the tanks again. That should be fun."

"You need *fun* in your life, John," Carol said over her shoulder as she walked out the cabin door. "We'll be heading out soon. Make an egg sandwich for Allen."

***

"Miss Carol, this is fun!" Mike shouted from the back of the UTV. They were passing the burnt remains of the gas station and downtown Lake View. The blackened bones of Carol's Diner still a sad reminder of a past that would never be again.

"Fun?" remarked Allen. "Fun is me still being asleep. I was up most of the night on guard."

"I'm sorry, Allen," Carol said. "You can nap at my place while Mike and I rummage around and get the things I need. We'll probably be there for an hour or so."

"John said I had to be on guard."

"It will be fine, Allen. Take a nap."

"Yes, Ma'am, you're the boss's..." he stopped himself mid-sentence.

She glanced at him. "I'm the boss's *what*?" Carol asked, a slight upturn of a smile on her face.

"We all know you're the boss's girlfriend, Carol. That's all."

"Well, I hope you aren't listening to me just because I'm the boss's girlfriend."

"No, Ma'am."

"Good answer, Allen."

She pulled the UTV into the drive alongside her house. She parked next to the side porch that led into the kitchen. Not far away was a large detached garage and a shed to its side. Everyone hopped out and headed inside. "The couch in the living room is pretty comfortable, Allen," Carol said as she headed toward the door.

Allen slid off the UTV and looked around. "I should take a walk around first, Carol. I'm supposed to be your guard while I'm here."

"You make it sound like I'm a prisoner," Carol replied.

"Not at all, but I need to be responsible." Allen headed around the house to see if anyone had been there.

He has a point. She removed her Glock from its paddle holster on her hip. "Stay here a minute, Mike. I need to make sure no one has taken up residence."

Moving slowly inside the house, Carol checked each of the rooms on the first floor and then went upstairs to check the bedrooms. Coming back down, she went to the back door. "It's okay, Mike, no bears."

"Bears?" Mike said, his eyes getting big.

"Bears, like in *Goldilocks and the Three Bears*."

"Ohhh, that's funny, Miss Carol. I thought you meant real bears at first."

Allen searched around the house, looking across the unplanted fields. Walking out to the road, he looked left and right but saw nothing.

"Naptime," Allen said to himself as he stepped inside the house, lay on the couch and leaned his AR across him. Closing his eyes, he was quickly asleep.

"Let's go up to the attic, Mike. That's where I keep the good stuff," Carol said, pretending to tiptoe around a sleeping Allen.

"Ya!" Mike exclaimed, then quickly clamped his hand over his mouth as they headed up the stairs to the large attic with all of its treasures.

***

"Rog said we were to look around and report back," Shane said to the other two bikers. They both nodded their heads and continued riding toward what remained of Lake View. As they got closer to the town, one of the riders signaled Shane by pointing toward a house on their right. Parked alongside it was a UTV.

Shane motioned for them to turn around and go back. After they traveled a few hundred yards, he signaled for them to stop and shut off his bike.

"Looks like someone is in the house," one of the men said.

"Yeah, and we aren't supposed to start anything," Shane replied.

"That house has been empty for a while, Shane. I noticed that the last few times we came through. We should check it out. That looks like the UTV we saw yesterday," Archie, the other biker said.

"I don't know. Rog said not to start anything. He was pissed you pointed your gun at those people yesterday."

"Let me go up there and see what I can find out," Archie insisted.

Shane glared at him. "You're just gonna ride up on your bike all nonchalant and shit?"

"No, I'll sneak up, real casual-like. I'll make sure no one sees me."

"And if they do?" Shane asked.

"Then I'll tell them I'm lost and hungry, some shit like that."

"So help me God, if you *start* any shit."

"Relax, Shane, I got this."

Putting the kickstand down on his bike, Archie stooped over before he ran toward the house with a large belt knife slapping at his side and an AR in his right hand. As he got closer to the home, he stooped down even lower.

Almost at a crawl, he approached the front porch. He softly stepped up onto it, walking across the grey painted boards until he was next to the large plate window in front. Peeking in, he saw a living room, a fireplace on one end, a couple of chairs and a couch. He had to look closely at the couch before he realized someone was sleeping on it. Quickly pulling himself away from the window, Archie crept back down the stairs and headed toward the back of the house.

***

"What? Hmmm, what?" Allen said as he awoke. "Somebody here?" But no one was there.

Swinging his legs to the side, he put his feet on the floor and sat up to rub his eyes.

"I should go check outside," he said as he stood up, picked up his AR from where he had leaned it, and walked toward the kitchen and back door.

As he moved through the kitchen, he glanced out the rear window that was over the sink. He went to the door, stepping onto the side porch. Stretching his arms wide, he tilted his head back, yawned, and suddenly felt something poking into his stomach.

"Don't move one muscle, kid, or I'll blow your guts out," said a male voice.

Allen stood still, his head back with his eyes looking at the sky.

"Slowly come down the steps. Make a noise and you're dead."

Allen went down the three steps, and when he reached the gravel at the bottom, he heard, "Now, stop, and don't move. Give me this." The voice's ownerreached for and took Allen's AR from his hands.

"Head toward that garage," the voice commanded.

Allen followed the instructions. His feet crunched on the gravel as they walked up to a door at the front of the garage.

"Open the door and go inside."

Allen reached for the knob and went inside the garage.

***

"What's that fucking idiot doing?" Shane said.

He had been watching Archie through a pair of binoculars and saw him enter the garage with someone else.

"Dammit," Shane said. "C'mon, before that moron starts something we can't get out of." He and the other biker took off at a run, heading toward the house and garage.

As they reached the garage, Shane said, "Archie, it's us." And the two men entered the garage.

They immediately saw a young man on his knees, his hands behind his head and ankles crossed. Archie held the weapon, pointing it at the young man.

"What the fuck do you think you are doing?" Shane demanded.

"He came outside, and I had no choice," Archie explained.

"Well, tie him up and gag him. We have to go."

Archie didn't move. "I should just cut his throat and be done with it. Besides, there's a woman and a kid in the house."

"How do you know?" Shane asked.

"I'm not stupid. I got the kid to tell me," Archie replied, motioning to the young man with the AR.

Shane looked down at the young man and saw his eye was red and swelling.

Archie waved the AR again. "I knocked the shit out of him, and he told me."

As they stood there, the other biker tied up the young man and was stuffing a gag in his mouth when they heard someone yelling.

"Allen! Allen, are you out here? It's time to go."

"That must be the other kid," Shane said. "Make a noise, so he comes in here."

The other biker kicked a box, rattling its contents.

"Allen, are you in there?"

The accelerating steps of a young person running across the gravel drive could be heard from outside the garage.

Shane stepped aside just as a kid burst into the garage.

Reaching quickly, Shane grabbed the boy by the collar and jerked him back. A brief scream came from the boy as Shane put his hand over his mouth.

"Kid, you make another sound, and I'll gut you like a pig," Shane said through clenched teeth. "Not a sound. Do you hear me?"

The kid's large brown eyes shook with his head as he indicated he understood.

"Now what?" Shane said, looking at the other men with him. "You got us into this, Archie. You have any brilliant ideas to get us out of it?"

Archie grinned. "I guess we gotta take the woman now."

"Yeah, we'll have to now," Shane said. "Rog is gonna kick your ass."

Archie gestured again with the AR. "No, he's not. I bet these are the farmers that Brad's been bitching about the last few days. We could use them for trade, hold 'em for ransom. Rog will like that."

"Bring the kid. We'll use him for bait to get the woman," Shane ordered as he pushed the boy toward the other biker.

Throwing the kid over his shoulder like a sack, the biker joined Shane as they headed toward the house.

Before leaving the garage, Archie picked up a short 2x2 that was leaning against the wall, striking the gagged young man in the head twice with it. He slumped to the floor, bleeding, and unconscious.

The three bikers and boy entered the house through a kitchen and went into the living room.

Putting the boy down, spinning him around, and standing him in front of Shane, the other biker stood there, waiting for instructions.

Shane grabbed the front of the boy's t-shirt and scrunched down in front of him as he threatened, "You call that woman down here right now, but don't you dare tell her we are here. You tell her, and I'll kill you."

The boy was trembling, but doing as he had been told, he shouted, "Miss Carol!"

A muffled voice could be heard from upstairs.

"Again," Shane ordered.

Soon the sound of footsteps could be heard coming toward them. Legs appeared on the stairs, and then quickly stopped.

The woman saw the men and the boy standing in front of them. She reached for the weapon in her holster on her side and managed to get off one shot.

Two rounds from Archie's AR hit her in the chest, knocking her backwards.

Falling down onto the steps, the woman slid down. Gurgling could be heard as blood filled her lungs, and she fought to breathe.

"You shot Miss Carol!" the boy cried out. "You fuckers shot Miss Carol."

Slapping the boy in the back of the head with his hand, Shane said, "You don't talk that way, boy."

Turning toward the others, he said, "Pick him up, we're going back."

Rog is gonna be so pissed.

As they started to leave, Shane noticed a notebook on the coffee table across the room. Opening it up, he scrawled a message.

We have the boy.

***

Gary and Rick rode slowly, heading toward Lake View. Their trip to the Winstons had been successful. For a pair of horses, they were getting two sows and a boar, and one of the sows was over two months pregnant. By fall, they'd have new piglets and bacon. Tomorrow, they would go back with the wagon and trade the two horses.

The steady clop clop clop of the horse hooves on the blacktop was comforting. Gary had to fight to stay alert. The rhythmic sound kept lulling him into an almost hypnotic state.

"Gary!" Rick shouted. "Is that John's UTV at Carol's place?"

"Sure is. John and Carol must be there. Let's go give them the good news." *I hope we aren't interrupting anything that will embarrass them.*

Nudging the horses into a canter, the two men hurried to Carol's house.

Rick jumped out of the saddle while Gary mostly slid out.

"John, Carol!" Rick yelled as he raced up the back steps and entered the house.

As Gary reached the top of the steps, his body stiff from the ride, he heard a "NOOOOO!" and raced inside.

He found Rick kneeling on the floor of the living room, sobbing. "Rick, what…what's wrong?"

All Rick could do was point toward the stairs, tears streaming down his cheeks.

As Gary turned, he saw her. Carol was lying on her back, her shirt covered in blood.

He slowly went over to her, knelt by her side, and confirmed what he already knew. Carol was dead.

Sinking down onto one of the steps, Gary let out a long breath. *Dammit.* He turned and looked at Carol again. Her eyes were open as she lay there, and he closed them for her. *Dammit.*

Gary stood up and went to Rick, grabbing his shoulder and pulling him to his feet. Softly he said, "Rick."

Rick's tear-filled eyes looked at Gary, the question of why written in them.

But Gary couldn't answer that. "Rick, listen to me. She didn't come here alone. John would never allow that. We have to look around and see if anyone else is here."

Rick nodded his head and went toward the front door.

"Look around outside, check the garage and the shed. I'll look inside," Gary instructed.

Rick picked up his Remington and headed out the door. Racking the bolt, he made sure that a round was ready.

Gary surveyed the living room. Other than Carol's wound, there was no sign of a struggle. Then he saw the note on the coffee table. He picked it up and read it. *What boy? Who?*

Going toward the stairs, he headed upstairs, being

careful as he moved around Carol. Walking into the bedroom, he pulled Carol's white goosedown filled duvet off the bed and went downstairs, covering her up.

Just as he finished, he heard Rick shouting. "Gary, it's Allen."

As best he could, Gary ran toward the back door and out into the yard. "Rick, where are you?" he shouted.

"In the garage."

Gary ran into the garage, where he found Rick kneeling over Allen, bound on the floor and bleeding. "Is he…?" Gary asked.

"No, he's breathing."

Gary knelt alongside the two young men and checked Allen's pulse. "He has a good, strong pulse. There's a first aid kit in my saddlebag. Run and get it," Gary ordered.

Rick jumped to his feet and ran outside, returning quickly with a dark blue zippered first aid kid. Handing it to Gary, he said, "Is he gonna be okay?"

"I don't know," Gary said. "Get on your horse and go back and get John and Donna. Tell them to bring the truck, but don't tell them anything else. GO!"

Rick spun around and raced out of the garage. Jumping onto his horse, he galloped down the road and toward the Henry cabins.

Gary opened the first aid kit and slowly began to clean the wounds as best he could without causing more damage. He removed 4x4 gauze pads, which he placed over the wounds on Allen's head.

Allen's eyes suddenly popped open. "Mike! Carol?" he shouted. Then, his eyes closed and he was out.

He's still breathing, that's good.

Gary continued to clean the wounds and took the gauze roll and began to wrap the Allen's head to help stop the bleeding. *I hope this kid will be okay.*

***

Rick reached the drive and turned onto it, racing past the bunker and up into the yard. "JOHN, JOHN!" he shouted.

John shouted from the barn as he started to jog toward the cabin. "Rick, what is it? What's wrong?" he asked.

"We need your help! Gary said to bring the truck and Donna. Something's wrong at Carol's house."

"Shit!" John yelled. "Donna! Donna, grab your med kit. NOW!"

Racing from the garden, Donna ran up to join them. "What's wrong?"

"Gary needs us. Something happened at Carol's house. Get your bag, let's go. Rick, you stay here. Your horse is laboring from the run."

"But…" Rick said.

John ran for his truck without waiting for his answer and started the engine.

Donna ran to the back door of the cabin and a moment later came running out of the front door, bag in hand. She hurdled off the porch and ran to the truck. Together, they raced down the driveway, the engine screaming in protest as John accelerated as fast as he could.

***

Please, God. Please, God. Please, God, not now raced through my mind. As the truck tires left the dirt and gravel drive, they squealed on the blacktop, spun a second, and then grabbed the pavement as the truck streaked down the road.

"What's wrong, John? Did Rick say?" Donna asked.

"No, all he said was something happened, and Gary said to bring you and the truck."

"I hope it's not bad."

"Me, too, but I have a bad feeling about this, Donna. A bad feeling."

"Those voices talking to you again, John?" she asked.

"Yeah, something like that," I said.

I had always heard or *felt* things. My mom told me it was a family curse that went way back to our Poland ancestors, where her family was from. Right now, none of that mattered. I just had a bad feeling.

I pulled into the drive at Carol's, slamming on the breaks. The UTV was in front of me with Gary's horse tied to it. Before the truck even stopped, Donna had jumped out and headed toward the side porch. She stopped and changed direction when she heard Gary shout, "John, Donna, in here. The garage."

We both ran toward the garage and saw Gary cradling Allen's bandaged head.

"What happened?" she asked.

"What the hell happened?" I shouted.

Gary looked up. "I don't know. We rode by and saw the UTV. I thought it was you and Carol. So we rode up, and I found Carol inside. It's not good, John," Gary explained, his eyes welling up.

I'm not sure I heard the last part of what he said, but I must've. I turned and ran toward the house.

I heard Gary shouting, "John, no!"

I burst into the kitchen and yelled for her. "Carol! Carol!"

I headed toward the living room. There, on the stairs, I saw her. She was covered with her favorite goosedown filled duvet.

Carol's legs, covered by her cuffed jeans and the hiking boots with the bright red laces, told me everything I feared. I ran to her, pulled back the cover, and cried out in pain.

Gary told me later it was the most awful scream he had ever heard.

I don't know how long I sat there before I heard Gary's voice behind me. "John, John, there's more," he said softly.

I stared up at him, seeing him but not seeing him fully. I'm certain my eyes were red-rimmed and showed a whole lot of hatred. People had told me I could be very kind and gentle until something happened, and then my eyes would turn. The look in my eyes scared them more than anything they had ever before seen.

"John, there's more," Gary said. "It's Mike. Whoever did this took Mike."

I sat back on the steps, stunned speechless. The anger building deep inside me.

Gary saw it, too. "John, we have to act rationally. They wrote a note and told us…"

"Where's the note?" I interrupted. "Show me the note!"

Gary picked up the note from the coffee table, handing it to me.

I read it. **We have the boy.** And nothing more. "That's it?" I said angrily.

"That's all, John."

"Son of a BITCH!" I shouted. I crumbled the note in my hand as I balled up my fists. "This is not going to be easy for Brian or Nancy. They are going to go ballistic."

"John," Gary interjected. "Right now, we have to get Allen back to the cabin so Donna can help him. We need to take Carol home, and then we need to figure out what to do about Mike."

"I'll take Carol to the truck, Gary."

"Let me help you," he said.

"Not this time, Gary. I need to do this."

Gary walked away and left me alone with Carol. Sitting there, all I could think about was the last conversation we had before she left. I felt regret and sadness as I let the tears fall as I carried her to the truck.

***

"You fucking did what!" Rog yelled. He glared at Archie, but his anger was directed at both Archie and Shane. "What fucking part of *don't start anything* did you two not understand?"

"Rog, we…" Shane started.

"Shut the fuck up. I don't want your excuses," Rog exclaimed.

Turning toward Archie, he said, "I want your ass out of here now. You, your bike, and one rifle. Get the hell out of here. I should make you take that damn Brad with you, too. You're both more trouble than you are worth."

"Rog, I…" Archie said.

"I said *leave, now,* and don't come back," Rog interrupted him, his teeth clenched in anger.

Placing his hand on the Browning 1911 he had on his hip, Rog said, "I mean it, Archie, leave now."

Rog didn't wait for Archie to comply. He looked at Shane and said, "I put you in charge. You were supposed to keep something like this from happening. Now we have a war on our hands before we are ready, and trust me, dumb ass, there will be a war." Rog put both hands on his hips, his beard dancing on his chest as his anger swelled. "I'm going to give you a note. I want you and stupid shit there to take it to those people."

"I thought you wanted him to leave?" Shane asked.

"I need bodies, soldiers right now. If he disobeys, if he talks back, if he looks at me sideways, I'll shoot the fucker. You understand me?"

"Yeah, I understand."

"Now go bring that kid here, and I'll write the note. Then, I want you and Archie to find those people and give it to them. No need to wait for a reply."

Chapter 7

*"We should forgive our enemies, but not before they
are hanged."*

—Heinrich Heine

We got Allen back to the cabin, and Donna and Linda began to take care of him. Donna thought he had a severe concussion at a minimum from his injuries. She stitched him up, all 24 stitches for the gashes in his head. Shaving the area had been a bit challenging, but she'd managed with a pair of scissors and a couple of disposable razors. Gary and Craig made a pallet for Carol out on the porch.

Brian and Nancy were another story. It took everything we had to stop Brian from racing across country to find Mike. We almost had to tie him up. He was so angry.

Having spent a lot of time weight training and then with all the physical labor he'd done since the EMP hit, it took Gary, Sajan, Craig and I to settle him down. Now, he sat in my chair on the porch loading and unloading magazines in an AR. Thirty rounds pushed in and thirty rounds pushed out, over and over again.

I was at a total loss as to how I could help my son, but right now, there was nothing anyone could do. I sent Sajan out to the bunker in front to keep watch.

Nancy was out by the garden, madder than hell, and I was waiting for her to explode. It was inevitable, and I understood that. I didn't know whether to explode in anger or break down in a show of tears. I'm usually pretty strong in a crisis, sometimes to the point of being accused of being callous or cold. I'm neither, but this time felt different. This time I didn't know what I should do or how I should react. Mike was my grandson and been kidnapped. Carol had been the love of my life…

I shook away the pain. The best thing I could do was try and talk to Brian.

I felt awkward as I walked over to him. I wasn't sure how to comfort him. "Hi," was all I could manage.

He didn't say a word. He just stripped the rounds out and then pressed them back in over and over.

I tried again. "Brian."

"They are going to die. Every one of them bikers is going to die," he said in an eerily quiet voice. "I will kill every one of them."

I had no doubt of that right now. Brian would slay the world for his son.

Sam came over and said he, Linda, and Gary would take care of Carol, get her ready. They didn't have to say what for.

I didn't even reply to him. I just nodded and watched my son. "Brian, talk to me," I said.

"There isn't much to say," he replied. "I'm going to kill them."

"We will, son, but we have things we have to do first."

"Don't pull your *planning* bullshit on me right now, Dad. I'm not in a mood for that."

"You know that's what we have to do. They took him, and that means he's alive. Otherwise…"

I couldn't finish the sentence. Nothing needed to be said, the meaning was understood. Brian stood up and threw the full magazine out into the yard.

"MOTHER FUCKER!" he screamed.

And then the tears flowed. I wasn't certain what to do, so I hugged my son.

He tried to fight it at first, but then he gave in. He hugged me hard, too.

"We'll get him back, Brian," I said quietly. "We'll get him back, and they will pay."

Deep inside, I knew things were about to get real ugly. Inside all of us was the ability to kill, destroy, and become very deadly. If we weren't careful, we would get lost in the rage. Yet right now, I didn't care. These animals had harmed us deeply, destroyed what we loved. I was ready to become an animal, too. "You need to go to your wife now."

"I know." And reluctantly, he headed toward the garden and Nancy.

A roar startled me from behind as an HMWWV drove up into the yard. It was Rahn. It stopped, and he and Specialist Johnson got out dressed in their standard Army Combat Uniform known as ACUs. The ever-present SAW gunner, who I had learned, was Private First Class Schwartz, stood in the turret.

"Sajan told me you had some trouble," Rahn said, walking up with his hat in hand. "I'm sorry, John. I don't know what to say."

"Oh, you know what to say," I answered. "We all know what to say, and it's going to happen, too."

"You know you have to put the emotion aside. You can't race off chasing smoke and expect to find the boy."

I knew he was right, but reason and smart thinking weren't what I wanted to hear right now. I motioned for him to walk with me, and we headed for the tree line in the side yard.

"We're going to war, Chris. I'm ridding the world of these animals, and I'm doing it as soon as I can."

"I can help," he replied.

"Thank you," I said, and I choked up.

Rahn looked down awkwardly, giving me a second to regain control. Control that up to this point, I had not realized I hadn't had. I knew I would need it.

"What do you know?" he asked.

"You mean besides Carol being shot dead, a kid is inside with a busted head and maybe worse? My grandson has been kidnapped, and God knows what else they've done to him." The venom in my voice was obvious.

"I'm not the enemy here, John. I can help. I'm on your side."

"It's not your fight, but thanks, Chris."

"If it's that biker gang we've been hearing about, you don't have enough people. There are over 30 of them, mostly men and a few women. We think the remnants of that looter gang you took out joined up with them. You'll need help, and you know that. You need to think clearly, John." His voice was firm, but understanding. "Let's find out for sure. I'll bet they'll make contact with you. They'll want something, and that will tell you the who and where. Then, we can act." He patted my shoulder, and his touch brought me back to the present, my thoughts once again more positive.

"You're right. I know it. It's just that… It's too soon. I need to think, calm the hell down, and channel. Thanks, Chris."

He nodded the affirmative. "I'll see what I can find out. I came out here to tell you our instructions are to clean out Antigo and bring everyone there that's left in town in to the camps. We are to leave the farms alone. For now, seems the good major figured out we might need to eat fresh food when the MREs run out."

I squinted at him. "He say any more about me, us?"

"Oh, he brings you up often. I think it has more to do with me and that you took out the looters. Word travels fast, and your people are becoming heroes."

"Speaking of Antigo," I said, quickly changing the subject, "you know anything about a Haines family?"

"Haines? Hmmm. Don't know. What can you tell me?"

"Can someone get Linda please?" I yelled toward the porch.

Addie raised her hand and went inside. She came back out with Linda, pointed her toward me, and I waved Linda over.

"What do you need?" Linda asked. Like the rest of us, she looked tired.

"Linda," I said, "this is First Sergeant Chris Rahn of the National Guard. He was stationed in Antigo. You may want to ask him about your family."

"Good to meet you, First Sergeant," she said, extending her hand.

Rahn took it, shook her hand, and said, "Nice meeting you. I wish it were under different circumstances."

She shrugged. "It is what it is."

"You say that with some authority, Miss. Were you in the service?" he asked.

"No, and it's just Linda. I have a lot of friends and family." Stopping herself, she started again. "*Had* a lot of friends and family that were in the military. I did some work with veterans, too."

"I see. So tell me about your family."

"Sure. Helen and Richard Haines. They're my aunt and uncle. Older couple, live near the fairgrounds. My uncle was a Vietnam Vet and hung out a lot at the VFW."

"Sounds familiar," Rahn said. "Tall guy, huge sideburns, talked loud and had a big laugh?"

Linda smiled. "Yes, that's Uncle Richard."

"Miss, your uncle tried to stop some looters at the VFW. It didn't go well. They beat him up pretty bad. Me and Johnson there were driving by and chased them off, then took your uncle home. I'm sorry to say he didn't make it. I went back a few days later to check on the missus, a grey and red-haired lady."

"Yes, that's Aunt Helen," Linda interrupted, tears rolling down her cheeks. "Sorry, I'm... I mean, they are all the family I have left."

"Yes, ma'am. I'm sorry to tell you that I found her laying next to your uncle on the bed. Looked like she took some pills."

"Thank you, First Sergeant," Linda said quietly, her voice breaking. "I guess it's been a rough day for everyone." Turning away, she first walked, then ran back to her cabin, letting the screen door swing shut behind her.

"Christ, that was delicate, Chris," I said.

He glanced at me. "I don't know how else to do it, John."

"We've had a shit pot full of bad news today. This one will not be forgotten for a long time."

"No, I'm sure it won't. Anyway, I'm sorry to say that I may soon have orders to come get you. If we take out this biker gang, words gonna get back to the major. I'll be told to bring you in."

"I can't let you do that. We're taking them out, Chris, every last one of them.So I'll ask you again, what will you do?"

"Not sure yet. I know Johnson and I will help you with the bikers. I'll check with Schwartz, too. We just need to know when and where. I'll get some others, of that I have no doubt. Then, if I get the order to bring you in, I'll make my decision then.."

"Thank you," I said, extending my hand.

Rahn took it and said, "I need to get going. I'm sure Wolfe knows we are talking, but I don't want to give him too much to really know."

"I understand, Chris, and thanks again."

"You betcha. Let's go, Johnson," he ordered.

"Okay, Top," Johnson said.

"Dammit, Johnson." Rahn shook his head from side to side.

The vehicle stopped, and Rahn got out. Reaching into the bed of the HMWWV, he grabbed two duffle bags and brought them over. "Boots," he said.

"Thanks," I replied.

As he walked to the vehicle, he shouted, "Upward and Onward," climbed in, and they drove off.

I grinned, the first time in a while, as I watched them drive off.

It was quiet again. I don't know if I wanted it to be quiet. I stood there for a moment, collected myself, and then headed for the barn. Taking a deep breath, I realized I had a grave to dig.

***

Just inside the town limits of Lake View, Archie and Shane stopped, got off of their bikes, and talked about what they were going to do.

"How are we supposed to find these people, Shane?" Archie asked.

Shane glanced at him. "We'll find them. I'm thinking if we screw this up, you're probably dead."

"Rog didn't say that, did he?"

"What do you think?" Shane asked. "He was pissed, and you know it. You're lucky you're even here with me."

"So, what's the note say, Shane? Did you read it?"

"Nope, none of my concern. Rog said to find the farmers and give them the note. That's all."

"You aren't even curious?"

"I'm not reading the note. Just shut up before I shoot you."

Archie leaned back on the sissy bar of his bike. *Screw you people.*

Shane walked around in a circle. Several times he went by Archie, and several times he had to hold his hand up to keep Archie from talking.

His fingers played with the hoop earring he had in his right ear. He came to a stop, shuffled his boots on the road, and turning, said, "This is what we'll do. We'll drive by the farmhouse that's empty, but we'll stay on the road. I'll fire three shots in the air, and that should draw them out."

"What if they think we're shooting at them and they start shooting at us?" Archie asked, his eyes wide.

"Good question. Let's find a stick and a white rag. You can hold it up like a flag, just like they did in those old western movies. That should keep them from shooting at us."

"How do you know that'll work?"

"I don't. If it don't, then you get shot and I get away."

"Screw you, Shane. I ain't getting shot for nothin'."

"You'll probably get shot by Rog if I don't do it. But understand, Archie, I'm ready to shoot your dumb ass right now," Shane said. "Now, let's find a white rag or something that'll work."

After a few minutes of searching, they found a white kitchen towel someone had left on a clothesline and took off toward their destination.

***

The clatter of the field phone startled Linda and Donna as they worked on a variety of herbal remedies together. "It's the bunker phone," Donna said as she dashed out of the bedroom to answer it.

"This is Donna," she said.

"Donna, this is Sajan. I just saw two of the bikers racing down the road. The sound of their bikes stopped not too far away. I think they are in front of Rick's old place."

"I'll let John know. Thank you." Replacing the receiver, Donna went through the kitchen and out the side door, looking for John. Seeing Brian and Nancy sitting on the ground underneath the big tree by the garden together, holding one another, she called out, "Have you seen John?"

Brian pointed out toward the field behind the house.

"Thanks," she yelled to them.

In the distance, Donna saw the UTV and headed that way.

Just as she arrived, there came a distinctive BAM, BAM BAM! Three gunshots rang out.

"John, I..."

Dropping his shovel, John jumped into the UTV and started driving toward the cabin. Seeing her, he pulled up alongside Donna and shouted, "Get in," and continued driving toward the cabin.

"I came out here to tell you Sajan called and said he saw two bikers drive by," Donna said.

"The shots sounded like they came from Quint's place," I replied back.

"That's where Sajan said he thought they'd stopped."

As we pulled up to the house, Brian, Gary, Craig, and Sam were in the yard gearing up.

"Saw you coming. I thought we should wait till you got here," Gary said. "Someone wanted to dash off," he added, using his head to point at Brian and Craig.

"Thank you for stopping them," I said.

"Okay, listen up. As far as we know, there are only two of them," I said, glancing at Donna. She nodded her head in the affirmative. "Not everyone is going. Brian, I need you here to take charge."

"I'm going," he interrupted.

"I need you here, and that is where you need to be," I said the words more firmly.

Brian stood there, silent, staring at me for a few seconds before he went to the porch where he loudly sat in my chair.

"Gary and Craig, you come with me. I want everyone else here ready. If you hear shooting, come like the cavalry."

The three of us headed out. I could hear their charging handles being pulled back and released. We were as ready as could be.

It took us about five minutes before we saw two bikers, one holding a white rag on a stick. They were in the middle of the road. The one holding the rag didn't look too comfortable. He looked nervous in fact, and that made me nervous. Gary, Craig, spread out and stay here. They make any kind of move that you don't like, shoot 'em."

"John, we need one of them alive," Gary remarked.

"Then kill the one that makes the move that you don't like," I said.

The sound of my boots padding on the blacktop was the only sound as I stepped on the road. It was all I could do to keep the rage from overcoming me. As far as I knew, these two were responsible for killing Carol, beating up Allen, and taking Mike. Yet, I wasn't one-hundred percent certain, so that little bit of doubt kept me from killing them without asking questions.

I took my AR by it's pistol grip, finger on the trigger, dumb I know, and marched toward them. The weapon moved from one to the other and back again. I wasn't in a mood for foolishness.

"Where's my grandson?" I yelled.

As soon as the words left my mouth, I knew it was a mistake. But it was too late.

The man not holding the stick had a paper in his hand. "I'm supposed to give you this," he said. He took a few steps closer until we were about six feet from another. His hand was shaking as he extended the paper.

I took it from him, and as soon as I did, he started to walk away. "Where are you going?" I asked sharply.

"I was told to deliver it, so I'm leaving."

"I didn't say you could leave. You and your friend here, drop your weapons and kick them away."

The two men did as I said.

"I want you both to sit on the ground, NOW!"

The man dropped the stick with the rag on it, and both of them sat on the road.

"Put your hands on your head and cross your legs," I commanded.

As they complied, I shook the paper open and read it.

We have the boy. If you want him back safely, meet us in the field by the house where it happened in two days at noon. Don't try anything, or he won't be safe any longer.

I looked down at the one who gave it to me and asked, "You know what this says?"

"No," he answered. "I was just told to deliver it."

"Were either of you involved in this?" I pointed the gun from one to the other.

"No, we weren't there," the guy with an earring said. "Rog thought it best he not send one of them."

"Rog, that's his name. Rog?"

"Yes."

"Well, you give Rog a message for me. We'll meet him, and if so much as a scratch is on that boy, every last one of you is dead. You go tell him." I pointed my AR at the other biker. "He's staying here for insurance."

"Rog ain't gonna like that."

"I don't give a shit what Rog likes or doesn't like," I said. "Go get on your bike and tell him what I said."

The man stood up, dusted off the seat of his pants, and as he walked to his bike, said, "I told you, Rog isn't gonna like this."

"And I told you I don't give a shit."

"Shane, don't leave me here. Don't leave me," the other man said.

"Shut the fuck up, Archie," Shane replied. He got on his bike, started it, and drove away.

I heard someone running behind me. "Dad, why'd you let him leave?" Craig asked as he came up beside me.

"Because I have this asshole," I replied. I handed him the paper.

Craig read it and said, "We need to get with Brian, we need to…"

I stopped him. "Don't say any more till we get Archie here back and locked up. Then, we'll talk. Show the letter to Gary."

Gary had made his way out to us. Craig handed the letter to him. I told Archie to stand up, and we started to march him back to the cabin.

"What about my bike?" he asked.

"No problem." I turned around and unloaded my 30-round magazine into it. "The bike is now not a problem."

"Nooo… Oh shit, man," he said, "you can't…"

I punched him in the mouth. "No more talking."

When we got back, I told Craig to take him into the barn, strip him and tie him up real tight. Then, Craig was to meet us back on the porch.

***

"They kept Archie," Rog said. "That's classic. I should just return the kid and let them know Archie started this shit."

"Why would you do that, Rog?" Shane asked.

"This is our chance to stick it to them and get more supplies than we could ever imagine," Brad added.

"I'm not gonna do it," Rog said. "I don't like Archie, and it's his damn fault we have this problem, but I'm not turning down a chance to make a big score, either. So, we go through with the trade. If we lose Archie, we lose Archie. I don't care. We have two days. Let the boys party all they want, but the night before, everyone is a virgin. No parties, no drinking, no pot. Got it?"

"I'll let 'em know," Shane said and left to relay the news.

Rog and Brad commenced a staredown, neither flinching, neither averting their eyes. Both men stood there, glowering at each other.

Brad broke the silence first. "You look pissed. You said we'd do this."

"I am pissed, kid. I'm pissed at you. I'm pissed at Archie. I'm pissed at the fucking world. Get over it."

"We got this. Those farmers are going to pay."

"You better be ready. I don't want any of your weaseling shit for this. You and your little group better be ready, and *you* better not screw up."

"We won't."

"Where's the kid?" Rog asked.

"The women are watching him. Mike's too much of a smartass for the guys, and when they started talking about cutting off his ears and other parts, I figured we'd be better off having the women watch him."

"Go get the little shit," Rog ordered.

Brad left the room of Rog's headquarters, and returned with Mike a few moments later. Mike was still wearing the same green t-shirt, jeans, and Air Jordans. Brad was holding tightly onto Mikes's left arm, and Mike looked none too pleased. Brad slung him forward toward Rog.

Mike stumbled a bit and then stood in front of Rog. He didn't blink, he didn't move. He just stood there.

I think this little fucker's smiling.

"You can leave, Brad. I'll call you if I need you."

Without comment, Brad walked out of the room and closed the door.

"I hear you're a smart ass and are pissing off my guys," Rog said. He raised his voice, trying to intimidate Mike.

Mike just stood there, not saying a word.

"You're supposed to answer adults when they talk to you, kid."

"My dad and grandpa are going to kill you," Mike replied in a strong voice.

"Hmmph, I don't think so, kid. We talked to your grandpa. We're trading for you."

"My Uncle Craig calls you people fuckers. I'm not supposed to use that word, but I think he's right," Mike said.

"You have a smart mouth, boy. How'd you like it washed out with soap?" Rog was losing his temper. "BRAD!"

Brad opened the door and entered the room.

"Get this little shit out of here before I start cutting parts off of him. Lock him in the closet down the hall."

Brad grabbed Mike by the arm and started to drag him from the room.

"My dad and grandpa are going to kill you," he shouted as he was drug down the hall and tossed into the closet.

"You can rot in there for all I care, kid," Brad shouted at the closed door.

Mike could hear his footsteps as the man walked away. That was when he let the tears flow and buried his face in his arms.

Chapter 8

*"Healing is a matter of time, but it is sometimes also
a matter of opportunity."*

—Hippocrates

We got back to the cabin, and Craig had taken Archie into the barn, had him strip, chained him up using some logging chain and a couple of padlocks, threw him a scratchy horse blanket, and left him.

"How'd it go?" I asked him when he joined me and the others on the porch.

"He started to object, but that didn't last long," Craig answered.

"You didn't kill him, did you?" I asked.

"Nope, but he might not see too good out of one of his eyes for a while."

I had explained to everyone what had occurred in the meeting with Archie and the other biker, Shane. The note was passed around, and everyone had had a chance to read it. Tension filled the air at the unasked questions.

"We have a lot to plan for folks," I started. "Before we do that, we have something else to do. We have to…"

And then I choked up and had to pause. Pursing my lips, I gazed out across the yard and focused on the trees. I breathed in slowly to calm myself. "We have to bury Carol. I have to finish digging her grave."

Interrupting, Sam said, "Linda and I finished it, John."

It was a good thing I was sitting down. On the one hand, I was very grateful they had done this. Sam and I had both known Carol for years, and I know he felt her loss heavily, too. Linda was new, didn't really know any of us, nor did we know her, and it was a kind gesture on her part. On the other hand, I was angry. That was for me to do.

I guess everyone thought I was trying not to be emotional again as no one said a word. "Thank you," I managed to croak out.

Standing, I glanced around at each of them before I walked across the porch to where Carol still lay, covered with a shroud made from a bedsheet that had been sewn closed. It was still stained from her wounds, which was a stark reminder of how she died. I placed my hand on top of her head and thought of our short time together. How this must be some kind of cruel joke being played on me. That a woman I felt such a connection to was put into my life and then violently removed from it just as quickly. It was brutal, and it hurt. With my back still to the group, I announced, "Let's send her home."

Sam and Gary came over and each took an end of the stretcher that had been made for her. Everyone else, except for Sajan, who was still on guard out in the bunker, filed off of the porch and stood in the yard.

Sam and Gary carried her down the steps, and I walked behind them, at Carol's head. They took the stretcher over to my pickup and gently slid her into the bed.

I told Brian to drive, and we all followed the truck out into the meadow, past the new cabins. It took us no more than a few minutes to get to where Carol's grave had been dug.

Sam and Gary removed her from the truck. They had left a couple of long ropes that we rested her stretcher on and they gently lowered her inside.

The silence overtook everyone. No one said a word; we stood there, each in our own thoughts, each with our own feelings.

I broke the silence. "I'm not a religious man, but I'm a man of faith. It's my faith, and I won't burden anyone with it. So, I'll just tell you about Carol. Carol was the first person I met here in Lake View. Of course, I met her at her diner. She made me one hell of a burger. I think we clicked because we both were veterans."

The other veterans in our growing family nodded their heads. We had a bond that no one but us understood.

"Carol played a role in my finding this land, the land where she will spend eternity." I had to pause as my emotions were surfacing again.

No one said a word, no one moved. They waited for me.

"Through the years, our friendship grew, and we grew together. Carol became family, and she treated my sons as if they were her own. She was strong, independent, and vocal."

A few quiet chuckles were heard as memories of her opinion sharing surfaced.

"When all of this happened, Carol wanted to stay at her home. She told me that we had kept our relationship between us for so long that we should keep it that way until things began to return to normal. But when the diner was burned down, she had nothing to stay in town for anymore. So, she moved out here. As we all grew in our situation, Carol and I grew closer. Eventually, using the excuse of space, Carol and I publicly shared a room. I hoped that none of you had figured it out before then."

"Some of us weren't blind to your relationship, John," Gary said. "We knew, but felt it was your business and not ours."

I smiled. Keeping secrets in a small town had never been easy. Sometimes, even impossible. To have that kind of respect for privacy was an amazing thing in a small town. I went on. "As we got more crowded here, Carol and I decided it was time to out ourselves. So, as needs changed, it became obvious."

"Dad, she is the only person I ever saw who got

away with stealing your coffee and then asked you to get her some more," Brian shared.

"That is true, son," I replied. "Carol rarely heard a cross word from me and usually got her way. So, it is with heavy hearts that we are all here today to say good-bye to Carol. To send her to the Summerlands where one day we will all meet again. So, this is it…" My voice cracked. "Farewell, Carol, farewell until tomorrow…when we meet again."

I took in a deep breath and slowly exhaled. All of this seemed too surreal to be made up. Yet here we were, here I was burying the woman I loved. It was all very real.

I bent down and took a fistful of dirt. I remembered something from many years ago, from my grandfather's funeral, the first service I had ever experienced. It left a mark on me that has been there ever since.

"From earth, you were made, and to earth, you shall return." I gently tossed the dirt into the grave. I think the thud the dirt made as it hit her shroud will be with me forever.

Everyone else slowly filed by and did the same, each picking up a small handful of dirt and softly throwing it onto Carol's body. Even Linda's two boys, Caleb and Ethan, who really had no idea what was happening, participated. Their small hands were participating in what I feared would become a ritual too often repeated.

They all stood there for a moment, not certain what to do or say.

"I'll be fine," I said. "Just give me some time alone, please."

Brian offered everyone a ride in the truck back to the cabin. I could hear them behind me as they climbed into the bed. I heard the engine start and the crunch of tires on the grass in the field as they drove off. Eventually, the sounds of the truck was gone, and it was just me. Me, a breeze blowing through the tall grass, and an open grave in front of me.

I stood there a long time alone with my thoughts.

A few birds were starting to chirp, and the evening air began to come out of the woods. Finally, I let the tears flow for a love lost.

I stayed until dusk.

***

Later, I walked back to the cabin, and as I climbed the front steps, I could hear everyone inside talking. I didn't really want any company or to be social at the moment, so I sat in my chair, stuck my legs out, and laid my head against the chair back, closing my eyes. The talking and sense of family being enacted inside brought me an amazing amount of peace. For a few minutes, I was able to forget what we faced and imagined all was normal.

I must have dozed because I suddenly heard little voices that awakened me. Opening one eye, I saw Caleb and Ethan standing a couple of feet away, whispering to each other as they watched me.

I made a big production out of waking up with exaggerated stretching and a loud yawn. They burst into giggles as only little boys can and ran inside the cabin, the screen door slamming shut behind them.

A minute or so later, I heard the door creak open. Linda came out on the porch and approached me. "I'm sorry if the boys disturbed you, John," she said.

"They didn't bother me at all. They remind me of my own at that age."

"I told them to leave you alone; that you needed your peace right now."

"Oh, you didn't have to do that. I don't mind little boys and their chaos. In a good way, they help. Their carefree way of going about things. There is an innocence in little boys, it's hard to describe, but it's different. They're special. They being here, even if it was just to watch me, helped a great deal."

"I know it's hard," she said. "I've lost family, too. You try hard to get over it."

"I'm sure I will. In time."

"If you ever, um, if you ever need to talk, I listen pretty good."

"Thank you," I said. "How about you? Do you need to talk?"

"Probably. But I'm not going to right now. I watch you, John. You are in some ways like myself. Independent, stubborn, and you don't take any shit from anyone."

I chuckled. "I try not to. Brian and Craig give me plenty, and Carol..." I stopped.

"I understand. When I heard about Uncle Richard and Aunt Helen, it hurt. That's why I ran off like I did. I don't like people seeing me cry."

"I get that. But it also means we're human, and that means sometimes it's okay to cry."

"Just don't be a cry baby," we said at the same time and laughed. The shared laugh felt good.

"Thank you, Linda. I'll remember your offer. I don't like to ask for help, but I'll accept an offer if I need it."

"I don't like to ask for help, either," she said. "I'll leave you alone now."

As she turned to leave, I called her back. "Linda, would you please ask everyone inside to come out here? We have a lot to discuss."

"Yes, of course," she answered.

It took a few moments, but slowly, everyone started to shuffle out the door and onto the porch. This disturbed the dogs, exhausted from napping all day, and napping again because of that.

I waited until everyone was present. Donna was out in the bunker while Rick was in the back. We'd put Allen upstairs while he healed, and he was breathing good but out like a light. Donna said she didn't think he was in a coma but more unconscious in the stereotypical sense. The fact that he was breathing on his own steadily and didn't appear to be in any distress were all good signs.

"Folks, first off, I want to thank everyone again for today. I'm sure Carol appreciated it, and I think we all, well, I think we all showed we're becoming more family instead of a ragtag band of people whose paths have crossed. Anyway, you all know the problem, and when you look around at our little band, we have a bigger problem."

"What's that?" Brian asked.

"We are in serious need of people. We don't have enough people to take on the bikers. We don't have the firepower."

"Yeah, we do," Brian said.

He had that look, and I knew if I pushed it, we were going to have an argument. We didn't need that right now. So I let him talk.

"We have the SAW, grenades, some claymores mines, and we definitely have more ammo than they do. I'd say we have fire superiority."

"I don't disagree that we can put down one hell of a volume of fire on anybody right now, but we have people issues. We need at least three to four people here. Someone has to watch this place. Someone has to care for Allen, and those two little boys can't watch themselves. That only leaves seven people who can go up against thirty or more people. Thirty, Brian, and in that mix is Mike. It won't be a fire-free zone."

"Doesn't mean we can't plan and be prepared if things shake out our way, Dad."

"I'll give ya' that, son." He was right. We couldn't go there with one plan. I was just concerned that in his frame of mind, he might pick a fight at the wrong time. "So, what's your plan, son?"

"Here it is. First, they aren't giving Mike back without getting something. That piece of shit of a human in the barn isn't going to be enough. The other guy let him stay too easy. There is more to that story. I think they'll give him up and not bat an eye. They will want what we have—food, weapons, probably the women, vehicles, and whatever else they can get. They know who Mike is, and they can figure out the rest."

"Oh, hell no, I'll die first," Addie said. "I'll go down fighting because that isn't happening again."

"It won't happen because before I let it happen,

I'll be dead," Craig interjected. He went to Addie and put his arm around her. "I'll die defending you."

Addie put her arms around him, hugging him close, burying her face against him.

"You two love birds done?" Brian asked with a smirk.

Brothers, no matter how close always rag on one another, at least in this family.

"Anyway, we have to get to the site early. We have the advantage. We already know it. At best, if they even do this, they'll have somebody watching the place beginning that morning. We'll get there the night before."

"That's tomorrow night, Brian," Sam said.

"Yup, but we can be ready. We'll put Craig up in the attic with the Remington 700. He can shoot the eye out of a chipmunk with that thing at 300 meters. Sajan, we'll put you, Rick, and the SAW along the fenceline just past Donna's old house. There are a lot of blackberry bushes and branches there for good concealment. You can sweep the entire field from there. Dad, you and me will meet with the bikers and hear what they have to say. I don't plan on leaving without Mike, and if we let anyone else talk to them, they'll get suspicious."

I nodded in agreement.

"Gary," Brian continued, "you and Addie need to be in the copse of trees on the far side of the field. You can use the bump stock, a few claymores, and another AR to send anyone who tries to escape that way back into the killing zone that Sajan and Rick have. That means that Nancy, Linda, Donna, and Sam need to stay here. Nancy and Donna can take care of Allen. Linda can watch her kids, and Sam can guard and be ready if we need him to call in the cavalry on his HAM."

"The plan sounds good, but won't Craig need a spotter?" I commented.

"I don't think that will be needed. Once Craig starts shooting, if he starts shooting, then Sajan and Rick will put down their fire. That will drive them towards

Gary. Gary and Addie can then fire off the claymores and drive them back into the field where Sajan can continue to light them up."

"And what about Mike?" Addie asked.

"We have to make sure that he isn't in the line of fire, which means we have to get our hands on him before anyone shoots," Brian replied.

"We better have a good set of signals, and no one better be confused," Gary said.

"We will. I'll walk everyone through it multiple times between now and tomorrow when we get in place."

"And you and I are taking our friend Archie out to meet them, and hopefully get Mike back?" I asked.

"Oh, we're getting Mike back," Brian said, his reply firm.

"Does anyone have any questions for Brian now?" I asked.

"Yeah," Sajan said. "Do I get to practice with the SAW?" His infectious grin was displayed from ear to ear.

"I'll make sure you're an expert with it, Sajan," Brian answered. "Anyone else?"

"How are Addie and I getting claymores and grenades to our spot? And will we have single clackers for each one, or will we have a panel like we used before?" Gary asked.

"Personally, I'd want singles because it takes less time and you can arrange them, so you know which one is which. I'll leave that choice to you. As to getting them there, well, we'll use LPCs," Brian explained.

Gary, Sam, Donna, and I laughed at that.

"What's an LPC?" Linda and Addie asked simultaneously.

"Leather personnel carriers. Your boots," Brian said.

"Oh," Addie said.

"Any other questions?" I asked.

No one seemed to have any, so I told them all to go to bed or whatever they had in mind for the evening. "We'll meet again tomorrow to make sure everyone knows their roles. G'night."

As they headed off to their own space, I saw Brian and Craig huddling up in the yard. I was tempted to go and see what they were up to, but sometimes brothers don't need their dad around. Instead, I went inside, took a cigar from my hidden stash, and went back on the porch. Except for the dogs, everyone was gone. I was alone with my thoughts and a mixed bag of emotions.

***

Most everyone woke up around the same time. Linda and Brian, of all people, made breakfast. Scrambled eggs and pancakes, with some syrup I had that was reconstituted with water. We added some dehydrated butter to it for extra flavor. If truth be known, we could have lived on pancakes and eggs for about a year, just on what was stored up. The ever-growing chicken coop provided us with a few fresh eggs, and the plan was to build that up to about two dozen every couple of days. Finding extra chickens wasn't hard. Catching them and bringing them here was the real challenge. Over time, they'd also become meat chickens, too.

Gary explained over breakfast about the deal he had made with the Winstons for some pigs. He had planned on returning today, but that would have to wait for a couple of days. We had to get through this issue first.

After breakfast, the activity picked up. Brian took Sajan and Rick out in the field and began showing them how to use the SAW.

At first, I was concerned it might be too much weapon for them, but Brian was right, Sajan was level-headed and smart. Rick, while younger, had matured quite a bit since we first met him. He would not be firing the weapon and would be more of an assistant gunner and security for Sajan.

"The hardest part, Dad," Brian explained, "is going to be teaching them short bursts, so they don't melt the barrel down."

I agreed, as automatic weapons have a hypnotic effect on people, and it's easy to pull the trigger and let the rounds simply fly until the belt is done.

"I've got two 100 round belts for them to practice with. That should be enough. If they have to use them for real, they will get plenty of practice in the field," Brian said.

"I'm gonna go check on Gary." I started to leave.

"Dad," Brian said, "you don't have to check on everything. People know what to do."

"I know," I answered. "Old habits die hard."

I left him, Sajan, and Rick to continue their work.

When I reached Gary, he had one of the Claymore sets unpacked and was explaining how it worked to Addie. As I approached, I heard him say, "It's pretty much dummy-proof because right here," he pointed toward the curved front of the mine, "it says front toward enemy. You want to make sure that it is facing away from you."

"Hi, Gary, Addie," I said. "How's it going?"

"I love these things, John," Gary remarked. "A sweet 700 little kisses for whoever gets in front of it."

Addie raised an eyebrow. "A sweet 700 kisses, Gary?" Addie asked.

"Yup, 700 little steel balls just waiting to fly out and kiss whoever they meet," he answered.

"That's a lot," she said as her hand reached down and touched the olive drab-colored hunk of plastic that made up the body of the mine.

"How is everything going?" I repeated.

"Good," Gary said. "Addie is doing well."

"I like this mine. It seems so simple to use," Addie said. "Can we shoot one off in practice?"

"No, we don't have many of them left, and unless the good First Sergeant can bring us more, we'll have to learn to make our own," I said.

Cocking her head to the said, she asked, "How will we do that?"

"John has books and videos, Addie. I'm sure he has

instructions on how to make these out of two strings, a pocket knife, and a tin can or something."

Addie looked confused, but I laughed at Gary's attempt at humor. Some people didn't get the old TV show reference. Regardless, I thought his attempt, at least, was funny.

"John, you got a minute to talk?" Gary asked as he stepped away from their makeshift table.

I took that as I was supposed to say yes, I have time. I followed him. After we got a few feet away from Addie, I said, "What's up?"

"I'm concerned, John. We need more people," he said directly.

"This is all we have, Gary. What about asking the townspeople or the Winstons for help?" I asked.

"Almost all of the locals have left and went wherever—Wausau, or moved in with other family members. The Winstons are good people, and they may join us, but we don't have time to go ask them, tell them the plan, and see if they'll do it. We have 24 hours. We're spread too thin."

"That's the only hole in Brian's plan. We don't have enough people. I get it. But we play cards with the hand we are dealt with, Gary, we both know that."

"Craig needs a spotter. Rick and Sajan aren't experienced enough to be so critical to this. You and Brian are too close to the issue, and I'm holding up the rear to redirect a group of crazed bikers back into a killing zone with a teenage girl who still has some issues because of what she went through. We're a sorry lot to try and pull this off."

"Are you suggesting we give in, give them what they want?" I asked, my anger starting to percolate.

"No, not at all. I know we can't do that, it would only cause more trouble. All I'm saying, shit, John, I'm just concerned. I'm not telling you anything you don't already know."

I reached out, putting my hand on my friend's shoulder and gave it a squeeze. "I know, buddy, I know."

***

Rog sat on the steps to the building he was using as a clubhouse and his own place. Smoking a cigarette that had come from the farmhouse raid, he stared at his roughed up leather boots. The smoke from the cigarette trailed up from his fingers, his hands resting on his legs. *Damn that Archie, he got us into this. That fucking Brad is trouble, too, but he's at least paid his way.*

Standing, he took a final drag off of his cigarette and flicked it away. The cigarette tumbled through the air end over end and landed on the dirt. "SHANE!" Rog yelled. "SHANE!"

A moment later, Shane came trotting up. "Yeah, Rog, what is it?"

"Go get a couple of the guys, smart ones, the kind that don't make mistakes."

"Okay, then what?"

"Well, bring them here, why the hell else would I ask you?"

Shane darted up the steps and inside the clubhouse. A short while later, he came back out with two guys. Both had the traditional biker garb on. Dirty, greasy jeans, black biker boots, a t-shirt, and a sleeveless jean jacket with the gang's colors on the back. Both had scruffy beards that wouldn't win any contests for appearance reaching the same length of their shoulder-length dark hair.

"Okay, boss, there are," Shane said.

"Alright, listen carefully. I want both of you guys to ride over to the house. Shane will tell you where it is, and look around. Don't go in the house and don't drive around the yard. I want you to look around and see if anyone is there, has been there, or is heading there. Then report back to me."

"What are we looking for?" one of them asked.

"People, anything that looks like a set up. I don't want any surprises when we go there tomorrow."

Chapter 9

"Success, the thing that comes from an icy execution
and a hardened heart."

—John Henry

The next day, we all gathered on the porch. Brian and I would take turns driving everyone over in the truck and help them get set up. After we had everyone in place, we'd come back to the cabin. Our part, up to that point was easy. They'd have to make sure their positions were well concealed and that they were comfortable. I was certain that the bikers would scout out the place before they got there, so good concealment and no moving around was necessary in order to keep them from knowing our plans. All Brian and I had to do was get our prisoner and drive over before noon tomorrow and see what happened.

Brian and I decided we'd hide our ARs inside the cab of the truck and wear sidearms to the meeting. Once we were in the field, we would be the most exposed and vulnerable. I had no idea how any of this would go, and that bothered me a lot. I had no control over the events.

We loaded everyone up on the truck and drove off. Sam was on guard and would be till morning. He waved as we left the property. We arrived at Carol's, and Brian went over the brush pile with Sajan and Rick to help them set up.

Craig and I grabbed bags of claymores and grenades, Gary and Addie picked up their weapons and spare magazines, and we headed across the field to get them set up. We could have driven, but I didn't want the risk of tire tracks or worse, getting stuck out in the middle of the field. It was then that I realized we could have some control over the meeting.

"Craig," I said, "we need to be out here waiting for them. Otherwise, they could go anywhere. We have to make sure that the bikers are in the field of fire we set up."

"Yeah, I was just thinking that, too," he replied. "Let's help Gary and Addie set up and then get Brian. We can do something to mark our spot so that you can be protected and the others get a clear view."

We walked across the unplowed field, more like a pasture now, and entered to trees on the far side. Addie had become quite the trooper as she took some of the claymore bags and placed them on the ground where she thought they should go.

I moved them forward about 20 feet to give them more cover behind the mines. Plus, I was a bit of a busy body and was still having to put my mark on everything to make sure of the desired results.

Gary assembled the pile of grenades and magazines, and then we went to work aiming the claymores.

I had forgotten you needed to get on the ground and lay behind the mine to aim it through the peep site. While doing that, I reversed the shipping plug but didn't screw it in all the way as we had to put the cap into it and then test the connection.

As I was aiming, Addie uncoiled the wires from each mine all the way back to where she and Gary would be, running them close to a large tree they could hide behind. Once that was done, I removed the plug, inserted the blasting cap, and after putting a stick in the ground, wrapped the wire around the stick.

We all assembled behind the tree where Gary and I had everyone lay down. We then removed the shorting plug from the blasting cap wire, plugged it into the test set, which we had attached to the firing device, and tested each line.

The lights came on, so they were all good. We removed the test set from the firing device, connected the wire to the device, put the safety up, and set the firing device down.

"The mines are now armed. Don't touch them, Addie, until it's time to fire them. We don't need an accidental firing," Gary explained.

She nodded her head.

I could tell she was nervous, and that was understandable. I knew it wasn't the right way to do it when I inserted the plug into the firing device, but I was more concerned with the emotion of the moment and someone forgetting to do that if they needed them.

Addie and Gary moved back into the trees where Gary unrolled a poncho. "Here Addie, why don't you lay down and try to get some sleep. I'll take first watch."

"I'll try," she said, "but I don't know if I can."

Craig put his arm around her shoulders, and the two of them walked back to where the poncho was. Addie sat down, and Craig handed her the liner for it, and they talked in low tones. All I could hear was the murmur of their voices.

"You all set, Gary?" I asked.

"As ready as we can be."

"Remember, the signal for anything to start. It will be either me or Brian throwing both of our hands in the air. Then, all you have to do is be ready, should they head this way after Sajan and Craig start shooting. You know what to do then."

"We'll be ready, John," Gary replied as he turned his head and glanced back at the two lovebirds barely visible in the dark. "I'll try and keep her out of this, too."

"Good luck with that. She seems pretty determined to me. These kids are tougher than we think. Remember when we were that age, we thought we could conquer the world, take a shower, and go out for a beer afterward."

Gary chuckled. "Those were the days. I sometimes wish I was that young again."

"Me, too. My knees often think that as well." I extended my hand, and Gary and I shook. "I'll see you when this is over," I said.

"Yup," he replied.

"Craig," I said in a normal voice. Sound carries in the quiet darkness, and I was being cautious, so I didn't shout.

"Coming," he said.

He joined me, I waved, and he and I headed out into the dark field.

"Go get your brother," I told him, and Craig took off at a jog toward where Brian, Sajan, and Rick were sitting.

***

"Right here," Brian said as they approached the cluster of blackberry bushes, old leaves, and branches. He set down the two ammo cans of belted 5.56 ammo for the SAW and took a pair of tan workgloves out of his back pants pocket. Rick and Sajan did the same after putting down the SAW and another two cans of ammo. The trio began to push and pull a path into the patch of thorny branches and vines. It didn't take long before Sajan said, "Sweet."

"What?" Brian asked.

"There's like a pocket in here that we can kneel down in pretty good. I can see the field through the branches but can barely see the road behind us."

"Sweet," Brian said.

They transported the SAW and ammo into the pocket, laid out a poncho on the ground, and got everything set up.

"I'm going out in front. I want you to get behind the SAW and let me know how well you can see me. Then I'll move left and right. Tell me how well you see me then, too," Brian instructed.

He crawled out, stood up, bent and stretched his back, and walked about 20 feet out unto the field. "Can you see me?"

"Barely," Rick answered.

"Why?" Brian asked.

"It's dark," Sajan said as he stifled a giggle.

"Jesus Christ," Brian said under his breath. "Other than the dark, is there anything in your way? Can you see me."

"Yes," Sajan said, still giggling.

Brian moved left and right, asking the same question. They could see him. Crawling into the bushes, I sat with them and explained, "Now remember, the signal is either me or John waving both of our hands over our head. When you see that, find whatever group came with the biker gang and open fire. Nobody gets away, take them all out."

"Okay," they replied grimly.

The reality of what was going to happen was starting to sink in.

"Stay in the bushes here. If you hear anything roaming around, stay here, and stay quiet. The only time you leave is if you are discovered and in danger of being shot, or worse. Rick, you're Sajan's security. You are to keep an eye out to make sure you aren't discovered. When he starts shooting, you feed him belts of ammo. If you guys somehow use all of your ammunition, take the SAW, get out of here, and head out across country back home. Whatever you do, don't lose the SAW. Got it?"

"We got it, Brian," Sajan said. Rick nodded his head.

"Okay, you guys take turns sleeping—one asleep and one awake. I may be back, so don't let me catch you both asleep, you hear me?"

"We hear ya', Brian. We got it," they answered.

"I'm outta here. See you later."

Brian crawled out, stood up, and again stretched out his back. When he finished, he started to head back toward the truck when he saw Craig jogging toward him.

"Dad sent me. He wants us both," he said.

The two brothers left and started toward the middle of the field.

***

I could see them both in the dark as they walked toward me. It was dark, and I couldn't get too upset that they weren't hurrying. We'd been here for a while, and I didn't want to get caught out in the open when false dawn showed up.

Seeing my two youngest sons walking across a field in the dark, on the eve of a battle, was a humbling vision. I could feel the chill, and it wasn't the night air. I was going to be with my sons in the biggest battle we had ever faced. I was proud of them. When they got within hearing distance, I said, "Brian, Craig, I want to talk to you. I thought we needed to have better control over the situation."

"There isn't much we can do, Dad. We didn't call the meeting or name the location," Brian said.

"You're right, son, but we *can* dictate where in the field the meeting takes place. I think it's a good idea we mark the spot where we will be with something that looks natural. A stick, a couple of rocks, something that looks like it belongs there. We can then tell the others what it is and know what their fields of fire are. You and I will get here early and be waiting at that spot. That way, when the bikers show up, we dictate where exactly we talk or whatever the hell we're going to do," I explained.

"That makes sense," Brian said. "Pull a stick out of the bed of the truck, Craig, and stick it here. We'll tell Gary, Addie, Sajan, and Rick where it is. When we come back, we'll park the truck about 20 feet away and then stand where this stick is. We'll pull it out of the ground when we get here tomorrow to help keep them from suspecting anything."

Craig went and got a stick from the truck and shoved it into the ground. "Good?" he asked.

"Good. Stay here while Brian and I let the others know. When we come back, you can go up in the attic and get yourself ready," I said.

"Sounds good," Craig answered. "I'll just be here looking for targets."

Brian and I took off toward our two teams to explain to them what we had done and why. The three of us met back at the truck about 20 minutes later.

"You ready, Craig?" I asked.

"I'm ready, Dad. We got this."

"We better," I said. "Ok, let's go." I turned and walked toward the truck. Out of the corner of my eye when I glanced back I saw Craig and Brian give each other a bro hug. They exchanged a few words, and Brian met me at the truck.

Craig headed toward Carol's place and the attic where he would be watching everything.

I sat in the driver's seat for a minute staring at Carol's house. The vision of what happened there within my eyes.

"You okay, Dad?" Brian asked.

"Yeah," I said huskily. Not letting my sadness get to me, I started the truck and drove to the cabin.

***

The two motorcycles rumbled down the road in the early morning semi-darkness. Rick reached over and shook Sajan. "Sajan, somebody's coming down the road."

Sajan let his eyes adjust as he woke, then sat up inside the vine pocket.

They both looked toward the road. It only took a few seconds before they saw the bikers.

"Crap," Sajan said. I hope they aren't early."

The two bikers slowed down as they approached the house and then, after cruising by a short distance, sped off toward town.

"I wonder what's up? We don't have a radio to call Brian," Rick said.

"I don't know, but we better stay awake now," replied Sajan.

A few minutes later, they heard the bikes roaring back toward them and then race up the road toward where they had originally come from.

"That might be the scouts John was talking about," Sajan said with some authority.

"Do you think they'll come back?" Rick asked.

"I don't know, but as I said, we better stay awake now," Sajan said. He reached inside the small day pack they had brought with them and pulled out a couple of protein bars, giving one to Rick. They sat there in silence, munching on their meager breakfast, drinking tepid water out of canteens, and waiting, watching for whatever came next.

***

I never did go to sleep. Brian went inside to be with Nancy, and I stayed on the porch in my chair, alone with my thoughts. I was worried about today. This thing could go south quick if it didn't go as I hoped.

The sun had come up and was starting to drythe dew on the grass and bushes. I wondered how Gary, Addie, Sajan, and Rick were doing. They didn't have any shelter and were probably a bit damp. It was summer, but this was Wisconsin. The morning would be fall-like for people in other parts of the country.

The screen door creaked, and Linda came out on the porch. She sat in the chair next to me and said nothing. After a moment, the silence was too much, and I said, "Good morning, what brings you out here?"

"Morning," was her reply. She sat there, staring at her shoes.

"Not a morning person?" I asked.

"I'm just scared, John," she said. "Nervous and scared."

"Wish I could say everything was going to be okay," I said. Those words no sooner left my lips, and I realized I wasn't helping.

I glanced over at her. Her just-below-the-shoulder brown hair hung loosely, some of it covering her eyes. She was an attractive woman, even this early in the morning.

"Something wrong?" she asked, sitting up a little straighter and seeming self-conscious.

I guess my glance was more noticeable than I thought. "No, I just thought I could have said something more encouraging than what I just did, that's all. I hope I didn't upset you."

"No, I understand what's going on. I've been hiding and living with this for weeks, months. I know the danger."

"How's Allen?" I asked, quickly changing the subject.

"He woke up for a bit and seemed to know where he was. He smiled at me, said hi, and went back to sleep."

"I guess that's a good sign, then?"

"I'm just a Pharmacy Tech, but the medical training I've had, plus what Donna has taught me says it's good. His body is worn out from fighting, and he's recovering. I think he'll be okay. It's just going to take time."

"That's good, then. I could really use him right now."

"I coulda gone, ya' know," she said a bit testily. "I'm just watching him. Nancy and Donna are the ones really taking care of him."

"I couldn't let you do that. You have two little boys to take care of. If something happened to you, where would they be?"

"I know," she said, almost defeatedly. "I worry about them. This is no way for them to grow up."

"I'm a parent, too. I know what it's like to worry about your kids."

"I'm sorry, I didn't mean to snap at you."

"You didn't. Sorry if I made you feel like you did." I'd done more apologizing to people in the last few days than I had done in the last few years, and that wasn't me.

Neither of us spoke, content in our silence. A few moments later, Brian came out, his arrival announced by the creaking screen door.

"Morning," he said. "Did you get any sleep?"

Linda and I both said simultaneously, "No." Then we laughed, but I suspect for different reasons.

Brian smiled his devious smile, the way he used to smile when he was a kid. "Uh-huh." He smirked, and went and sat on the steps. His now ever-present AR resting butt down between his legs and his Glock hanging on his side. I noticed that when he sat down, he had pushed something away on the other side.

He turned to face me and said, "I'm ready. We need to get this shit on the road."

"In a couple of hours. We should try and eat something first."

"I'll make some scrambled eggs," Linda said, getting out of the chair. "Is there any cheese?"

"There is down in the basement," I said. "A couple of small wheels of cheddar. Just scrape the mold off of it if it has any. It will be okay."

As she headed toward the door, she commented, "You sound like my aunt and uncle. They always said that." The door creaked again, and she went inside.

"Cute girl," Brian said.

"You're married. Stop it."

"I'm married but not blind," he replied. "So, are you ready for today?"

"I'm as ready as I'm going to get. Still nervous, though."

"We aren't coming back without Mike, Dad. I don't care how we do it. We are bringing him home today."

"Yes, we are," I said.

Then we both sat there in silence, waiting on what was coming and waiting on breakfast, too.

***

"We didn't see anything, Rog," one of the bikers

reported after they got back to the camp. "There was nothing there by that house. No cars, people, nothing."

"That's good," Rog said as he finished his cigarette. "Go get Brad and Shane. We need to get ready."

They ran off, and a few moments later, Shane and Brad showed up.

"We need to take everybody who has a bike and a gun. Brad, you're going, too. You can ride bitch with one of the guys. Shane, you bring the kid. They need to see him. I want them to know what's at stake here."

Brad stood there, his anger obvious. He said nothing as he clenched and unclenched his hands. "Why do you disrespect me so much? I've pulled more than my share," Brad said.

"Kid, don't get all jumpy on me or you'll get your ass beat. This is partly your fault."

"I didn't take the kid," Brad said sharply.

"No, but your beef with these farmers didn't help. Now we have to go through with this."

"Are we gonna trade the kid off, Rog?" Shane asked.

"I don't know. I want stuff. I want things they have. Weapons and food," Rog said.

"What about that girl?" Brad interrupted.

"You want the girl you *ask* for her," Rog said, getting his face inches away from Brad's.

Brad backed down and dropped his eyes.

"Now start rounding the guys up, Shane. Get 'em armed and bring 'em here. I need to set the rules."

"You got it, boss," Shane answered and headed off across the camp.

***

"It's time, Dad," Brian announced as he walked up on the porch.

I set my coffee down on the floor, stood, grabbed my AR, and followed him to the barn.

Going into one of the middle stalls, we found Archie laying on his side on the floor. He was naked as the day he was born with a scratchy old wool blanket around him. A heavy logging chain was padlocked around his waist, up around his neck with another padlock, and between his legs almost diaper like. The other end padlocked to one of the big 4x4 posts that acted both as studs for the walls of the stall but also as supports for the upper level of the barn.

Brian walked into the stall and kicked Archie's feet. "Get up," he said in a none too kind voice.

Archie stirred and sat up. "What?" he asked.

"I said, get up. Get dressed," Brian said as he tossed Archies' dirty clothes at him.

"What about this?" Archie asked, holding the chain in front of him.

Brian left the stall and went to get the keys for the padlocks, which were hanging on a nail in another stall far from Archie's reach. He returned, and as he approached Archie, he remarked to me, "If he even looks like he is going to try anything, shoot him."

"No problem," I said.

Brian undid the locks, Archie got dressed, and then Brian used a couple of zip ties to secure Archie's hands behind his back. He took an old rag, shoved it in Archie's mouth, and using duct tape, wound the tape around Archie's head to hold everything in place. "No talking asshole," Brian said.

Archie glared at Brian.

We put Archie in the bed of the truck, tied him to the spare tire, and then got in to head toward Carol's place. I felt determined, and the look on Brian's face was equally so.

As we drove past the front of the cabin, Linda and Nancy were out front. They waved at us as we drove by. In the bunker was Donna, and she also wiggled her fingers at us. The truck tires hit the pavement, spun for a second with a squeak, and we headed toward town.

***

"Listen up," Rog shouted. "I want everybody to stick together. When we get to the farm, we're driving out into the field and waiting for these farmers. When they get there, they will have Archie. I don't want anyone starting anything, that comes later."

He was interrupted by a chorus of laughter from the gang in front of him. Waiting till they finished, he continued, "Shane will have the kid. We will let them see the kid, maybe even talk to him. I want every one of you looking mean and hungry. No talking, shouting anything until I say so."

"Rog," Shane said in a questioning tone.

"Yeah, what?"

"How will we get the stuff we want if we give them the kid?"

"We'll make them go get it," Rog explained. "Now mount up. It's time to go!" Rog shouted to the 25 or so armed bikers. "Go get the kid, Shane. He rides with you. Don't drop him." Rog laughed as he walked away to his bike. *That's all we need, the dumb ass dropping the kid and making a slick spot in the road.*

***

The crunch of gravel under the tires of the truck was almost louder than the engine noise the truck had. I drove behind the house, then turned across the yard between the house and garage heading toward the field.

"Is he up there?" I asked.

Brian craned his neck out the side window and looked up toward the attic. From the round attic window with one glass quarter pane broken out, a hand waved. "Yup, he's ready."

"Good. Craig is our best security out there. Anything that looks risky or threatening happens close, and he'll know what to do," I said.

We drove out into the field, stopping about 20 feet from the stick. Brian hopped out of the truck, walked over to the stick, and kicked it flat off the ground. As he was doing so, we heard the roar of engines.

Less than a minute later, we saw them cresting the hill on the road about 100 yards from where Sajan and Rick were concealed. As they cruised by, I started counting, "Looks like somewhere between 20 and 30," I said.

"I counted 25," Brian remarked.

Damn sons, always have to correct their fathers.

I went to the back of the truck, untied Archie from the spare tire, and told him to get out. I then walked him over to where Brian was.

We stood there and watched the bikers, some taking the exact same route across the yard that we had. They rode out towards us and then drove in a circle around us before stopping as a group almost exactly where I wanted them to, but more like 30 feet or so from where it would be ideal. But it was good enough.

Archie tried to move, and I squeezed his arm. "Try it, and you're a dead man," I said through gritted teeth.

Brian and I stood with Archie between us. We both had our legs slightly splayed. Brian had one hand on his Glock and the other on what I had discovered was an issue KaBar I had given him before he went to Iraq. All he ever said to me after that was it had been used as intended.

I had my left hand on Archie's bicep and my right on my Glock. Our ARs were inside the cab of the truck, about twenty feet away over open ground. If we had to run for them, it would be dicey at best.

It was then that Brian and I both saw Mike. Like an electric shock, the reality of the situation went through us both. I know I felt it.

"Fuck," Brian whispered.

He felt it too.

Mike saw us. "Grandpa, Dad!" he shouted.

The biker he was with said something to him, and he quieted. But the little shit managed to wave. It was at that point I knew we were going to get through this.

A big burly man got off one of the bikes. He stood

next to the man with Mike. He wore a jeans jacket with patches covering most of it and bare-chested under it. His upper body and arms were covered with tattoos. He had a beard that went halfway down his chest. As he turned and looked at the other bikers, I thought, *this is the one that wrote the note.*

He walked out into the middle of the space between us, put his hands on his hips, and said, "I'm surprised you came alone."

"Give me my grandson back, and I figure we have no need to involve anyone else," I said.

"That the boy's dad?" he asked, the tilt of his head pointed toward Brian.

"Yup," Brian said.

"The boy talks a lot of shit and has no respect. You need to teach him some manners."

Brian started to say something when out of the corner of my mouth, I said to him, "Easy tiger. Not now."

My son actually listened to me.

"Hello, Archie," the biker leader said.

Of course, Archie couldn't talk right now, and I wasn't about to let him. "Are you going to make this trade and back off?" I asked.

With great theatrics, the man put his hands on his hips and started to rock back in forth in obviously exaggerated laughter.

"We aren't backing off, farmer boy," he shouted back at me. "I want half of what you got. I want half your food, half your weapons and ammunition, half of everything."

He no sooner finished, then one of the other bikers ran from the gang and approached him. Flailing his arms, I could hear him arguing about something. The biker leader pushed him away, and the other biker went back to the rest of the gang.

"You have a girl," he shouted. "She ran away from the kid there. He wants her back."

"I don't know who you're talking about," I yelled back.

"I think you're lying. We may have to see where you live and search for ourselves."

"I want to talk to my son," Brian yelled. "We aren't doing anything until I talk to my son."

The biker leader stood there, clearly thinking about it. He stroked his beard a couple of times and then yelled, "Shane, bring the boy up here to talk to his daddy."

Another biker, short guy, and the same man we talked to in the road grabbed Mike by the arm and forcefully walked him forward. Mike was on his tiptoes as the biker brought him to us.

Brian started to move toward the biker leader.

"Easy there, partner," the leader said. "Come up slow like."

Brian slowed his pace but still walked quickly, stopping about 3 feet in front of the leader.

Mike and Shane came up close, standing between the biker leader and Brian.

"Here's the kid, Rog," Shane said.

"Rog," Brian said. "Interesting name."

"Talk to the boy, *Daddy*," Rog said sarcastically.

"Hi, mijo," Brian said.

It was a word I had heard him call Mike on occasion. It was Spanish slang for son. Where Brian learned it, I never knew.

"Hi, Dad," Mike said, squirming a bit as he tried to get out of Shane's grip and go to his dad. "Ow, you're hurting my arm," he said to Shane.

"Stop hurting my son," Brian said.

"He needs to stop squirming," Shane replied.

It was then that it happened.

I don't believe I have ever in my life seen my son move so fast. Out of nowhere, the kabar was in his hand. He shortened the gap between him and the biker, Shane, and almost decapitated him with a left-to-right slash of the blade.

Grabbing Mike by the arm, Brian dropped to the ground, pulling Mike down with him. It was then that I saw a cloud of pink mist followed by the BAM of a rifle shot.

Rog jumped as Brian grabbed Mike. He quickly looked around, not certain what was happening just as his head exploded into a mass of pink mist and gray brain matter.

I instantly knew what my two sons had been discussing. Brian was getting his son back.

"God dammit, Brian," I yelled as I began to wave my hands over my head. It took an eternity, probably about two or three seconds, but it seemed like an eternity before I heard the steady rapid-fire staccato from the SAW.

"Slow it down, Sajan," I heard Brian shout as he picked up Mike and dashed toward the truck.

I spun around and saw Archie kneeling on the ground next to me.

"Fuck it," I said aloud. I pulled out my Glock and shot the biker in his ear. Then ducking at the waist, I ran toward the truck.

Mike and Brian were on the far side of the truck. I was about five steps behind them when a sharp pinch grabbed my butt, and I fell to the ground.

I didn't slow down as I quickly low crawled behind the truck next to them.

"Getting old, Dad, if you can't run without falling down," Brian said as he used his body and the back tires to shield Mike.

"I didn't fall, dammit, I got shot in the ass," I shouted back.

The rate of fire from the SAW had fallen into a pattern of short bursts, and then an explosion rocked everything.

"Is that Gary?" I shouted.

"No, one of the motorcycles just exploded," Brian replied.

I crawled around so I could see in the direction of the bikers and saw black smoke and flame coming from one of the bikes. Quite a few of the bikers were on the ground, not moving. Others were shooting toward us and in the direction of Sajan and Rick. The roar was deafening, and every now and then, I'd hear a BAM and I knew it was Craig's Remington taking out another biker.

Then a few more explosions happened and I realized he was shooting the gas tanks on the bikes, causing them to catch on fire and explode.

About 10 or so of the bikers hopped up and ran for motorcycles, kick-starting them and taking off toward the back of the field. About 20 seconds after they did that, I heard BOOM, BOOM, BOOM, as either Gary or Addie fired three of the Claymores. They had two more, and I was glad Gary wasn't using all of them.

***

Thump, thump, banged through the hard shell top of the HMMWV. "What are you doing, Schwartz?" First Sergeant Rahn yelled.

"Did you hear that?" Schwartz yelled from his position, standing in the turret.

"Slow down, Johnson," Rahn said. "Hear what, Schwartz?"

"Explosions and gunfire. It sounds like it's coming from up ahead near Lake View."

"Shit," muttered Rahn. "Put the pedal to the metal, Johnson."

"What?" Johnson asked.

"Speed up, go fast, get to Lake View ASAP."

"Roger, Top," Johnson said with a grin.

The HMMWV lurched forward with the loud sounds of the engine masking what Rahn was saying. "Don't call me Top, Specialist Johnson."

***

"Shoot, Sajan, shoot," Rick yelled.

He had seen John wave his hands as well as seen Brian grab Mike. What seemed like an eternity swirled around both Sajan and Rick. Rick shouting at him, and Sajan realizing he had to pull the trigger.

When all of the parts came together, Sajan's muscles obeyed, at least the one in his finger as he squeezed down on the trigger.

Ratatatatatatatatatat. The SAW burned through almost an entire belt of 200 rounds.

"Slow *Down*, Sajan," Rick shouted.

Sajan let go of the trigger, stopping the weapon completely. Putting his finger back on the trigger, he did as Brian had taught him. Taking a few slow breaths, he began. *Pull and count to three, release. Pull again and count to three, release.*

As he did so, he traversed the weapon back and forth, left to right and back again, chasing the bikers as they ran helter-skelter around the field, shooting at what from here seemed like nothing. Sajan kept shooting at them as they fell and tumbled like bowling pins.

As quickly as it started, it ended and he couldn't see them anymore. They were on the ground, and some, he had seen, got on their bikes and escaped.

***

"Can you see anything, Gary?" Addie asked. The nervousness in her voice was obvious.

"Not yet," he replied as he watched the meeting through his binoculars, standing well inside the shadow of the trees.

Seeing Brian and two bikers talk in the middle of the field, he was puzzled when he saw Brian lunge toward the biker holding Mike.

KARAAACK! The sound echoed around him, and he saw a large second man go limp and fall.

"Oh, shit. Addie, get ready!" he exclaimed. It was on.

***

Addie went to the tree and reviewed the steps she was supposed to follow. Push the safety down to arm the firing device and squeeze the handle down as aggressively as you can until the blasting cap detonates. *Rinse and repeat,* she remembered Gary saying.

She sat there, praying to herself that everyone was alright. She knew the rifle shot came from Craig, and he was fine up in his perch. He had confided in her what he and Brian had planned. She knew John would be angry, but Craig had told her not to tell anyone.

Now it was real.

Craig had started the fight by taking his shot. The rapid-fire of the machine gun armed by Sajan had announced itself, first as a steady roar and then in short bursts. She could also hear the weapons the bikers fired. A mixture of sharp cracks mixed with deeper booming sounds.

"Get ready, Addie," Gary said loudly.

She reached down and picked up the first firing device. She wasn't sure if it would be the right one, but she and Gary had worked out a simple system numbering them from one to five, running left to right. She prayed her new family would survive this fight.

***

Gary stood, watching the group of bikers running toward their motorcycles. As they mounted them, the sound of revving of engines could be heard. The deep rumble of the Harleys reverberating around them.

"Shit," he muttered again.

He continued to follow their movements, fearful they'd run straight into the unprotected position he and Addie were in. The bikers began to veer to their right, and that was when Gary said, "Three, Addie, three."

She put the device down she held and moved over to the third one and repeated the arming process.

"When I say fire, Addie, you fire three. Then, pick up two and fire two, then pick up one and wait," Gary instructed.

"Okay," she said.

He could hear the nervousness in her voice, but he had faith in Addie. He watched the bikers as they got closer.

"Fire, Addie. FIRE!" Gary shouted.

Addie squeezed with everything she had.

BOOM! The first claymore fired, startling her.

Dropping the firing device, she picked up the next one.

BOOM! She dropped that one and picked up the next. Before she realized what she was doing, she squeezed the handle on the next device.

BOOM! It fired.

"CEASE FIRE! CEASE FIRE, Addie!" Gary shouted.

"I'm sorry, Gary," she said. "I guess I got caught up in all of the excitement."

"That's okay… I think we got them all anyway," Gary said.

Not wanting to trouble her, he turned away and put the binoculars up to his eyes. He smiled. *These kids are going to be alright.*

***

As soon as the shooting started, Brad dropped to the ground. Bullets were whizzing over his head as he crawled away from the conflagration that was building all around him. He felt something wet cascading over his body, and as he tried to brush it away, he felt something thick and sticky. It smelled like metal.

Glancing at his hands, he saw they were covered with something red. *Is that blood?*

A body fell on top of him, causing him to shout in fear. *This is not good.* He kicked and pushed the body off of him.

He continued to crawl away, passing by wounded people begging for help and being followed by the cold, vacant staring eyes of the dead.

Crawling away from the field, he could see a fenceline off in the distance, and as fast as he could crawl, he made his way there.

As the battle raged behind him, he rolled into a ditch that ran parallel to the fence. The vile smelling muck and water resting at the bottom of the ditch almost made him gag.

As he started to get up, he heard the sound of an engine and remained pinned to the ground as a military vehicle sped by him. He waited a minute for it to pass before he jumped up, running across the road.

Across another field, he saw woods. He'd make his way there.

***

Specialist Johnson raced down the road. Schwartz became an extra set of eyes for him as they headed toward Lake View.

"I can hear the rattle of firing up ahead now," Rahn remarked. "Slow down a bit, Johnson. We don't want to jump into a firefight and not know who is who."

"You know who it is, First Sergeant. It can only be one group, and you gave them the SAW I keep hearing," Johnson said as he backed off on the accelerator as he moved down the road at a pretty good clip.

"I can see activity in the field up ahead, First Sergeant, off to the right about 50 meters beyond the edge of the road," Schwartz yelled down.

"Slow down, Johnson," Rahn commanded. "The first chance you see, head into the field. I think I see Henry's truck out there."

Johnson didn't reply, but after driving about 15 yards, he made a right turn, bounced around and through the drainage ditch that ran along the road, and entered the field. He stopped when they came alongside the pickup truck.

Not seeing anyone but dead and wounded bikers a bit further away, Rahn stepped out of the vehicle and shouted, "John. John! Where are you?"

"Right here," came a voice from the other side of the pickup truck.

Rahn moved around the back of the truck as Schwartz, being vigilant up in the turret, traversed the field with his weapon ready to fire. As he rounded the back of the truck, he saw John lying on his stomach with a large wet spot on the left cheek of his butt. Brian was sitting on the grass with Mike, who looked a combination of scared and amazed.

"Did you get shot in the ass, John?" Rahn asked.

***

"Geez, not what happened. Not are you alright? You have to ask me the obvious, if I got shot in the ass," I said none too happily.

"It was the tear in the jeans that gave it away," Rahn said. "Be grateful I'm an observant First Sergeant and didn't think you'd shit your pants."

It was at that moment that I realized it was that strange quiet you hear about after a battle. The only sounds were the ringing in your ears and the moaning of the wounded. I realized I was lucky. A butt wound, while typically painful, wasn't life-threatening as long as it didn't get infected.

"Johnson," Rahn shouted. "Bring the first aid kit. We have a wounded man here."

"And don't you forget that, either," I said none too happily. If Rahn was going to bust my chops over being wounded, I was going to be a difficult patient.

Johnson came up with the first aid kit, and seeing me on the ground said, "Are you alright, Mr. Henry? Oh, you've been shot in the ass. That hurts, too. Happened to a friend of mine in Iraq."

"Fuck you, Johnson," I replied.

"Mr. Henry, I've got the pain killers. Be nice," he replied.

"And I told you people it's John. Doesn't anybody listen?"

"Relax, John," Rahn said. "Now, what in the hell happened here?"

"You should probably ask Brian over there," I grumped. "This seems to be the plan he and his brother concocted without telling anyone."

"Chief, what happened? And before you begin to tell me, know that I'm going to have to say something to the flagpole back in Wausau. You can't hide something like this, and people will talk."

While I got taped up, Brian spent the next half hour explaining the note from the bikers, how he came up with the original plan, and later, how he and Craig changed it if certain things happened.

"I knew we had them beat on firepower. All we had to do was get the leader, which Craig did, and then we could create havoc with the rest of them. I'd get Mike back, we'd get revenge for Carol, and we'd eliminate the threat."

As he explained all of this, the others started to arrive. Craig, Sajan, and Rick were first on the scene.

"Man, was that you that shot that guy, Craig?" Rick asked.

"Yeah, it was me," he replied.

"That had to be 200 yards."

"More like 250 to 300, Rick," Craig corrected, his chest puffed out in front of his brother.

Stopping his explaining for a moment, Brian came over, hugged his brother, and said, "Good shooting, little brother. You were spot on."

"I couldn't miss," Craig said with no modesty. "If I had, you'd rag on me forever."

"We should stop gabbing. You guys need to go over there, police up weapons and take care of the wounded," Brian said.

"Gentlemen," Rahn interjected, "that means give the wounded first aid."

"Yes, First Sergeant," the three boys said as they marched over to where all the bodies were.

"First Sergeant, you wouldn't think..." Brian let the question hang unfinished.

Rahn said nothing in return. Both men were combat veterans. They knew what could happen when people got their blood up.

As the three went toward the carnage of the field, I heard a "CRAIG!"

Addie and Gary had joined us. I had not heard any gunfire from their direction, just three claymores detonating, so I was confident they were okay.

Addie and Craig reunited on the field in a hug accompanied by a long kiss. Rick and Sajan encouraged them by woo hoo'ing and clapping.

Gary came up on us, dropped the bags for the two unfired claymores and the wire and detonators for the three that had been fired. He saw me lying on the ground and said, "John, you've been shot."

"I'll be okay," I responded.

"Oh my," he said. "You've been shot in the ass." Those words no sooner left his mouth, and everyone started to laugh.

"We should get you back to the cabin for better treatment, John," Rahn said. "We have to talk, too. It's why I came out here."

I agreed.

They loaded me up as best they could in the Hummer and took me home, along with Mike. Brian stayed with the others to clean up and come up with a plan for body disposal. If we didn't do that, it was going to get very smelly in a few days.

From what Gary and Craig said, it looked like maybe four or five got away, and those men were on foot. That meant we had about twenty-some bodies to deal with. I would worry about that later. Right now what was important was that we had Mike back, none of our people were harmed, and Carol had been avenged.

Chapter 10

*"Never anger Momma bear. The outcome will not be
to your liking."*

—Nancy Henry

The ride back to the cabin was painful. Hummer's
were not exactly Cadillacs with super gentle
suspensions. The bouncing around in the bed was
excruciating and uncomfortable. Nevertheless, Rahn
got me home. Donna and Linda finished patching me
up. Once they'd finished, and Nancy fed everyone—
after hugging Mike half to death and kissing him to the
point that he squirmed and complained—Rahn came
in to talk.

"Feeling any better, John?" he asked.

I could tell he was laughing. "I am until the lidocaine
wears off." My well stocked medical supplies were
once again paying off. I was laying on my good side—
cheek—and he sat in the only chair in my bedroom
across from me.

"Hydrate and take ibuprofen, John, hydrate and
ibuprofen."

"That shit still isn't funny," I said, and we shared a
laugh. It had become the mantra of pain management
for the army. Keep yourself hydrated, and let ibuprofen
take care of any aches and pains.

"So, what do we need to talk about?" I asked.

"Major says you have to come in," Rahn said.

"I already told you, that ain't happening." My tone
was a bit testy.

"That's what I told him," Rahn answered. "He said it doesn't matter. Plus, he's concerned with the violence out here, and you seem to be in the middle of it."

"I can't argue with him there, but we didn't go looking for it. Hell, Chris, we stopped it."

"I know."

"So, what's going to happen?" I asked.

"You know I have to report the fight with the bikers. The fact that some got away is concerning."

"I agree," I said, interrupting him. "Are you going to enforce his ruling?"

"Nope, can't do it. As it is, I'm ready to leave and take people with me. The three camps in Wausau alone are about a half-step away from being concentration camps. What goes on there that I know of is disgusting."

"Why don't you hurry up and decide, so you can help with your cabin?" I asked, halfway serious.

"I've already decided. We'll be here. It's *when* that is still up in the air. I want a few more guys with me, plus we—you—need more supplies. Ammo, weapons, stuff like that."

"How much can you get?" I asked, giving him a sideways glance.

"If I'm lucky, and I mean real lucky, a 5-ton's worth. Most likely, a trailer's worth or two."

"Don't get caught, Chris."

"If I do, it's a firing squad, and before you ask, there have been executions. Too many as far as I'm concerned."

"How much time do we have?"

"Worst case, a week or two, maybe less. Best case, a few weeks to a month. He wants it done now, but he needs more manpower to pull it off. Some FEMA troops and National Guard from Madison are coming up in a few weeks. When they get here, it's game on."

"That's not a lot of time. We can't stand up to a trained and well-equipped force, even *with* the Winstons. We'd have to go guerilla, and with winter but a few months away, we won't survive," I said.

"Even with what I can bring, it will be tough but we can do it."

"Have you ever heard of the Swamp Fox?"

He shook his head. "No, I don't think so."

"American Revolution, South Carolina, Francis Marion. Took on the whole British Army in the state, and won."

"We may have to go in that direction, John." He looked away for a moment, clearly thinking before he made eye contact again. "You heal up, and we'll talk when I get back up here. Watch the rock pile, worst case. I'll leave a message there. Sam's HAM radio isn't good. They know it's here, and they're monitoring it."

"Okay, thanks for the heads up. Stay safe, and we'll see you soon." We shook hands, and he left.

Linda and Donna came into the room shortly after Rahn had gone. "How are you feeling, hero?" Donna asked.

"My butt's numb. It feels like a brick," I said.

"It will feel that way for a little bit. Then the lidocaine will wear off, and you'll be more uncomfortable," Donna said. "Plus, it will itch, and you can't scratch it." She gave me a stern look.

"You say that like you enjoy it, Donna," I said rather snarkily.

"No, you just should know better. Running around, getting into fights is not something a man your age should be doing. You're lucky this wasn't worse. The bullet put a 4-inch tear in your butt cheek. Poor Linda here had to squeeze it together while I stitched it."

Linda's giggle softened Donna's anger.

"It's a really nice butt, John," Linda remarked with a smirk.

"Oh my God, seriously," I said. "You two are now rating my butt? Get out, both of you."

They both left giggling like a couple of thirteen-year-old school girls.

Brian had to squeeze past them as they left as he tried to get into my room. He pulled the chair over alongside the bed and sat down. I was pretty certain the look on my face let him know I was not pleased.

We sat there with our eyes locked on each other for

probably a minute or two, saying nothing. I'm often a talker, so staying quiet for that long wasn't easy. If what I was thinking came out of my mouth, the argument would be epic. My saving grace would be I could claim shock from being wounded, but I didn't think that would get me far. So I literally bit my tongue and stared at my son.

Finally, I had to say something. A thousand words of saying what raced through my brain. I chose the easy one.

"Just what in the hell were you and Craig thinking?" I barked.

"We got Mike back, everyone else is back, and the bikers are no longer a problem."

"Uh, huh. And what if it was Mike laying here shot instead of me. Did you bother to think of that."

"It went exactly as Craig and I set it up, Dad. Sajan and Rick knew some of it, and I told everybody not to tell you. So get mad at me."

"I *am* mad at you. That wasn't the brightest idea you've ever had."

"It worked, though. We'd of ended up doing it anyway. You heard them. They wanted our stuff. They wanted to make us their slaves. You know damn good and well, you wouldn't have allowed that. I know I wouldn't. Stop acting so damn high and mighty. You aren't the only one here making tough decisions and possibly getting people hurt or killed."

He stood up, pushed the chair further away from the bed, and started to leave the room.

"Stop!" I yelled.

He stopped but didn't turn around. He just stood there looking at the closed bedroom door.

"Are you going to stand there, or are you going to turn around and talk to me?" I asked.

Brian turned around, grabbed the chair aggressively, plopped it down close to the bed again, and sat. "We can talk, just don't talk to me like I'm a child, Dad."

Again, I bit my tongue.

***

Brad had been stumbling through the woods ever since he ran from the field and crossed the road. While he felt lucky to find the concealment that it offered, he felt unlucky because concealment also meant a tough environment. He was desperate and scared after what he had witnessed and experienced out there on the field. He still had other people's blood on him, and the stink from the ditch as all that muddy water soaked into his clothes lingered. He'd been scratched, bleeding from several wounds, and had provided a good deal of his blood to more mosquitoes than he ever hoped to experience.

Even though the temperature was warm, he was cold from being soaking wet. All he had for protection was a six-inch belt knife. It was the only thing he had thought to bring with him. He'd intended it for the girl. She was responsible for the death of his friends Sheri, Frank, and Carl. Her escape caused them to die.

And then he smelled it. It wasn't him.

It was food.

He could smell someone cooking food. *I haven't eaten all day.*

Stopping as much to catch his breath as to try and figure out what direction the smells were coming from, Brad could hear a noise in the distance, seemingly off to his right. People noises.

Before he started, he took a minute to check out his surroundings. He'd been up here in these woods long enough to know that everything wasn't always as it seemed, and while you may think you're alone, you may not be.

Convinced he was alone, he made his way slowly toward the noises he heard in the distance. He stopped every now and then to make sure no one was watching or following him. He let his ears tell him as much as his eyes did. The problem was, he was starving, and whatever was being cooked up ahead was seriously driving him mad. His stomach gurgled in protest as the effects of what Brad was smelling made his hunger more pronounced. It seemed like an eternity as he moved methodically through the woods, trying not to trip over tree roots, branches, rocks, or any other detritus lying around the forest floor.

Up ahead, he could see what looked like a break in the trees. He heard what sounded like kids laughing and playing—*the farmers.*

Brad dropped to his hands and knees and slowly crawled toward the edge of the woods. He stayed well inside the tree line so that he would not be easily seen by the people near the cabin. Across the yard, he saw three kids playing, two young boys and the kid that had started all of this. The little smart ass with the big mouth. *Rog shoulda just capped the kid and let it go.*

The three boys were running around, playing tag. Around the corner of the cabin, he saw a woman in jeans and a t-shirt tending a garden. Brad knew there were others here someplace. He just didn't know where.

Settling down in the bushes, he chose to watch and wait. Even though he was starving, his stomach protesting as it rumbled non-stop. Brad crossed his arms over his stomach and rocking back and forth, tried to end the hunger pangs.

As he sat there, two men walked out of the house. One man headed toward the barn. The other, a tall guy wearing camoflouge, went over to a military vehicle he hadn't seen, got into it, and then it drove away.

I better pay attention.

He continued to watch, holding his stomach and thinking through what he would do. The cooking smell appeared to come from a building that had smoke coming out of it that wasn't far from where the woman in the garden was. After a while, she picked up a basket that had been by her feet and walked toward the cabin. He lost sight of her after that.

The kids continued to play, and Brad concocted a plan. He had to eat, or he'd starve to death. He'd worry about the girl later.

138

***

Nancy had taken the basket of fresh herbs into the kitchen. She had basil and oregano, and her thought was to use the spices to make spaghetti sauce. They had some ground venison that she could brown up and add sauce to.

I need mushrooms. Then realized that most likely, she would never hear the end of the complaining. Brian and Craig didn't like the vegetable and she wasn't sure about everyone else.

Going inside, she searched for other ingredients that could add flavor. There was still garlic left, and she diced some up and added it to the mix.

The sauce was slowly bubbling in a large steel pot on the stove. She chopped the herbs and added them to her concoction, tossing in a little salt after tasting the sauce and finding it lacking. There was a large supply of dried spaghetti noodles in John's cache in the basement. Heading that way, she left the kitchen. It was then she heard the kids screaming.

It wasn't a good scream.

***

Brad ran from the woods toward where the boys were playing. Just as he grabbed the one he wanted and clamped his hand over the kid's mouth, the other two started screaming. Brad held the squirming and kicking kid, taking all of the energy he had left to hold on to him. He backed up toward the woods as a woman came out of the cabin. She was armed with a shotgun.

"Put my son down," the woman shouted as she limped toward him. She held the shotgun in her hands and pointed it at him as if she knew how to use it.

"Dammit, I said, put him down!"

"I just want something to eat," Brad shouted.

"Put him down," she shouted again as she came closer to him.

Brad knew she wouldn't shoot. The shotgun could hit the child.

"I just want something to eat," he yelled again. Brad remembered the boy's name was Mike, who continued to squirm and kick, making it harder for him to hold on to the boy as he backed closer to the woods. "Stop it, Mike," Brad shouted. *If I can get to the woods, I can drop this kid and run.*

In all of the excitement, Brad looked at the woman and all across the yard in front of the house.

I have to get away from here, but if I drop this kid, she'll shoot me.

He could see two men running from the barn heading his way, and another woman had just come out of the front door with a pistol in her hand. Brad was feeling desperate and began to realize he had made a terrible mistake.

***

Nancy inched closer and closer to the man as Mike continued to try and get away.

"HOW DO YOU KNOW MY SON'S NAME?" Nancy shouted. "How do you know *his* name?"

Mike was kicking and flailing his arms, twisting his body, and doing everything he could to escape.

"I'll put him down, just don't shoot!" the man shouted.

The words no sooner left his mouth, then Mike twisted himself and broke free of the man's grasp. He began to run toward Nancy. And tears flowed down her cheeks as she scooped him up into her arms and hugged him tightly.

***

Stunned for a second, Brad stood motionless. Out of nowhere, a black and white streak slammed into Brad, knocking him to the ground.

Brad had enough time to throw up his left arm in an attempt to block the savagery hurdling toward him. A snarling and gnashing of teeth made Brad scream as he felt the flesh being torn from his arm. He reached for something, anything to help him fend off the attack.

***

Grady, Mike's Great Dane, had come to the rescue. The dog threw his 175-pound body into the man who was hurting Mike, and showed no mercy. As gentle as Grady could be with Mike, he would destroy what was hurting his littermate. Nancy stared, not knowing what to do except hold Mike tight to her.

The man managed to reach his belt knife. As he took it out of the sheath, he twisted his arm and stabbed at what was causing the pain, thrusting the knife again and again.

The dog snarled, biting his target more fiercely. Then suddenly yelped loudly, going limp across the man's body.

An eerie silence ensued.

The man pushed the dog off of himgrunting as he did so. Getting to his feet, he stared at the dog. Then, just as he started to turn, a shot went off and he fell to the ground.

BOOM!

Nancy had taken aim and shot him.

The man tried to crawl toward the woods, but she couldn't let him get away. "Mike, stay here."

She ran up to the man, screaming, "DON'T YOU EVER TOUCH MY SON AGAIN!"

"I just wanted something to eat," he said.

"I don't believe you. You tried to kidnap my son. You killed my dog. Eat this," Nancy said fiercely as she pointed the shotgun at him.

BOOM!

Craig and Gary reached Nancy just as she fired the last shot. The bloody mess on the ground wasn't moving anymore.

Gently, Gary reached over and started to take the gun away from her.

She wrenched it away from him, turning to point it again at the body on the ground in front of her.

"Nancy, it's okay," Gary said. "He isn't going to hurt anyone ever again."

A loud smack sounded from the porch.

Nancy startled and turned.

Brian, rushing out the door, pushed it so hard it swung back and hit the wall, disconnecting the spring from the door.

That movement had distracted Nancy and Gary was able to get the shotgun away from her. She stood there, trembling in anger.

"Mom," Mike yelled. He rushed to her, wrapping his arms around her, holding on as if for dear life.

She dropped to her knees and embraced Mike just as Brian got to her side.

"Nancy, are you okay?" he asked, astonished.

Nancy didn't respond. She continued to hold Mike, tears streaming down her face.

Donna had followed Brian and stood next to Craig, her pistol in hand. "What happened?" she asked.

"Looks like this guy tried to grab Mike," Gary said.

Angrily, Brian asked, "How the hell did he get here, and no one saw anything?"

Before anyone could answer, Mike screamed, "GRADY!" He ran over to the limp form lying on the ground.

"Oh, Grady," Mike cried again and again, and began sobbing.

"Nancy, somebody, get him out of here," Brian said. "He shouldn't be here."

Nancy crawled over and embraced her son, holding him tight as she rocked back and forth.

Between sobs, Mike repeated the name of his dog. "Grady, Grady, Grady, oh Grady."

***

"How did that man get here?" Brian asked.

Craig shrugged. "He must have come out of the woods. He looks like one of the people from the biker fight earlier today," Craig said. "He definitely looks familiar. I've seen him before."

Brian walked over and kicked the limp bleeding mass on the ground in front of him. About half of the man's face was missing courtesy of Grady, but he did look familiar. "Yeah, I've seen him somewhere. Maybe you're right, Craig. Doesn't matter. He's just a pile of garbage now."

Brian glanced away and looked at his wife and son, rocking on the ground, both in tears, Nancy trying to console the boy. Not far away, Grady lay motionless on the ground.

Brian went and kneeled beside Nancy and Mike, putting himself between them and the dog. He hugged them both as his eyes welled up with tears.

Everyone else had joined them on the lawn, except John. The entire yard was a mess of emotion. Nancy, Mike, and Brian huddled together, sharing their grief. Craig's anger was ebbing and flowing as his eyes watered.

Linda was kneeling with her two boys, consoling them over Grady's death, hugging them and trying to make them feel safe. Donna and Gary stood side by side lost in their own thoughts.

The only ones not there were Addie, who was on guard in the front, Rick, who was on guard in the back, and Sajan and Sam, who had gone to Rick's old place for more materials for the new cabins.

Brian went over to Grady. The dog was still on the ground, blood oozing from his fatal wounds. *He looks as if he is sleeping.*

Brian reached out and put his hand on Grady's head. The dog was still warm to the touch, and Brian squeezed him gently as if not to wake him. Warm tears cascaded down Brian's face as his grief grew. *You done good, Grady. You protected our boy.*

***

The loud creak and slamming sound of the door had startled me. Before that, the noise, then the screaming and the gunshots were too much. They resulted in my hopping out of bed, grabbing my Glock, and slowly making my way from the bedroom to the door.

Standing on the porch, I saw everyone milling about. Some on their knees hugging and others just standing there. The clatter of the field phone inside the door told me the guard positions were manned.

As I limped and hopped across the porch and to the steps, I heard Linda say, "John, you've torn out your stitches, and you're bleeding."

I heard her, but I didn't react to the words. I continued my hobbling to the yard to my son's family when Gary stopped me.

"Everything will be fine, John," he said in a soft voice. "One of the bikers apparently made his way here and tried to snatch Mike. Grady stopped him, and Nancy shot and killed the man. Grady didn't make it."

"*Jesus*," I hissed. I continued to head toward Brian and his family, but a tug on my arm stopped me. *Poor Grady. Poor Mike.*

"You've torn your stitches out and you're bleeding through your clothing."

It was Linda. The look of concern as well as determination on her face made me quickly look back at my wound. My shorts were blood-soaked, and blood was trickling down the back of my leg.

"Shit," I muttered.

"Let me get you back inside and cleaned up," she directed as she led me toward the cabin.

Grudgingly, I went with her.

***

Linda stitched me up and doted over me like a mother

for the next few days. I was starting to itch back there, and Linda told me that it meant I was healing. I wish I could say the same for Brian and Nancy. They were not doing well, the stress of the last several days obviously the cause. Brian told me they'd made a space for Grady near Carol. He didn't say, and I didn't ask what they'd done with the biker, but I assumed they'd dug a hole for him, too. The state of the world had made a lot of people desperate.

Donna had pretty much left Linda to caring for me while she took care of the now fully awake and wanting to get out of bed, Allen.

I didn't need any caring for and was probably the worst patient Linda could have. There was no danger of my pulling the stitches out anymore. Because I had, I was apparently going to have a scar "worthy of many conversations." Why I would show anyone, much less talk about a scar on my butt was lost on me. Nevertheless, Linda showed a stubbornness I hadn't experienced from anyone in a long while. When she made up her mind, that was it, as I was quickly learning.

Gary and Rick had left to scout the surrounding areas and head to the Winstons. All was calm, until they returned with pigs and news from the Winstons.

Chapter 11

"If I am forced to choose between having to betray my country and betraying a friend, I hope I will have the guts enough to betray my country."

—Chris Rahn

"First Sergeant, my office," Major Elias Wolfe said with as much authority as he could muster. The six-foot-tall, curly brown-haired and rather young infantry officer was all business as he walked into his office and waited for Rahn to report.

Rahn entered the office and stopped. He was instantly corrected.

"Is that how you report to a commissioned officer, First Sergeant?"

Chris Rahn, experienced at this little game the Major was obviously intent on playing, came to attention, marched to the front of Wolfe's desk and saluted. Holding the salute, he said, "First Sergeant Rahn reporting as ordered." He held the salute until Wolfe returned it.

Wolfe wasted no time in getting to the point. "I heard your friends, the Henrys, had a bit of trouble."

"Yes, Sir, that is what…"

Interrupting him, Wolfe said, "I wasn't asking for an answer, First Sergeant. I already know about the altercation. I have other soldiers that are more forthcoming about telling me things."

The pause was deafening in its silence, but Rahn remained stoic.

"I understand they had automatic weapons and possibly even claymores. Do you know anything about that?" Wolfe prodded.

Rahn stood there, quiet, waiting for the major to demand an answer from him.

"You can answer now, First Sergeant."

"A lot of people have automatic weapons, sir," Rahn said. "They aren't illegal with the right permits."

"I don't need a flip answer, First Sergeant," Wolfe sneered. "I had the local records checked, and no records exist for the licenses or permits that Henry would need for an automatic weapon."

"I don't know anything about that, Major. Maybe he got them from somebody who had a permit or took them from someone he had a disagreement with out there. Mr. Henry is rather creative and resourceful."

"Your admiration for him is rather telling. That is troubling to me. I warned you about this."

"Major," Rahn said firmly, "I don't know anything about Henry's automatic weapons. Maybe he has some old bump stocks or something. Maybe it's like I said, they were found or taken. I don't know. I don't know anything about the claymores, either."

"As far as I'm concerned, he is in possession of illegally obtained explosives and automatic weapons. You will put a platoon together and go up there, confiscate those weapons, and return here. I want him with you. Oh, and that warrant officer son of his, too. It's time for the chief to return to military control."

Good luck with that.

Rahn kept his cool. "I don't know, Major. The way I see it, he hasn't broken any laws, and the incidents that I am familiar with are all in self-defense. There isn't a lot of law enforcement there, And we don't have a permanent presence up there so…"

"I'm getting the impression you are disobeying a direct order, First Sergeant," Wolfe said. "This isn't a debate. We are under martial law, and this isn't a democracy," Wolfe explained.

"Major, I'm not aware of any declaration of martial law," Rahn interrupted.

"As of 1000 hours this morning, we are. Came down from headquarters in Madison."

"The governor declared martial law?" Rahn asked.

"The governor is no longer in office, nor is the lieutenant governor. The regional FEMA executive is in control."

"With all due respect, Major, that doesn't sound exactly legal."

"I don't care about your opinion, First Sergeant. We are under martial law and you will follow orders, am I understood?"

"Yes, Sir."

"Now do as you are ordered," Wolfe said.

"Yes, Sir."

"Close the door, First Sergeant."

Rahn turned and closed the door. He then returned to the front of Wolfe's desk and stood there casually.

"Chris, this is a big deal," Wolfe began in a friendlier tone. "We have the chance to rise to the top here and be real leaders in the rebuilding of this country. A lot of things will change, shoot, a lot of things *have* changed. It's time to go along with it."

"Yes, sir," Rahn said.

"Now, everyone out there," Wolfe used his head to point toward the closed door indicating the outer office, "heard your words, and they heard mine. You've had your say, and now it's time to play the game. So go out there, follow your orders, and bring Henry in. Bring both Henrys back here."

"Yes, sir," Rahn said. He saluted, and the major returned his salute.

"Dismissed, First Sergeant," Wolfe said calmly.

Rahn executed a sharp about-face and exited the major's office, closing the door behind him.

I need to find Johnson.

***

Gary and Rick arrived at the homestead. We had started calling it "the homestead" after the extra cabins had been built. It sounded better than Fort Henry, which had been suggested but I promptly rejected. They pulled up in the wagon, and inside it was two sows, half a dozen piglets, and one real angry boar.

"I thought you were getting two sows, a pregnant one, and a Boar," I said from the porch where I was parked on top of a bunch of pillows.

"Charlie said he felt bad about everything we'd been through and how he couldn't help us, so we got six piglets extra," Gary said.

"That was decent of him," I replied. "What did it cost us?"

"Same deal I made originally. Two horses and a foal, if one of the mares we have here have one."

I wasn't thrilled about giving up new stock, if and when we ever had any, but the pigs were a good deal. With the piglets, we could more easily breed and not worry about any defects. We'd be fine for some time. "Okay, thanks for taking care of the deal."

Craig, Allen, Sajan, Mike, Rick, and Gary each took a piglet out of the wagon and headed toward the barn where we had built a pen.

That was when it happened. My dog, Max, saw new playmates. He'd been a bit depressed since Grady died, and he heard the squealing piglets and went over to play.

Max knocked over Craig first, who promptly dropped his pig. The pig started running, and Max then knocked over Sajan, who was trying to get to the running piglet.

So now we had two piglets running around, two men chasing them, a dog going nuts with his new friends, and the others laughing. That's when Allen, Rick, and Gary started dropping their pigs. To his credit, Mike did not drop his until everyone else had.

About this time, King decided it was time to play, too. It was a sight to see two German shepherds, six piglets, and five adults and a child running around the yard. And on top of that, all of the humans started laughing, which made catching the piglets even more difficult.

My first thought was that if we ever had a county fair, none of these people would catch the greased pig. They were doing their best but failing miserably. Linda's two boys got in on the fun, which because of their age, was mostly just chasing the pigs.

Nancy came out of the cabin to see what the ruckus was all about, and spoilsport that she is, started yelling at everyone to "catch those damn pigs and stop playing around." Donna joined her, glaring at the situation.

It was right about that time I started laughing. Poor Mike, just like his Dad, always getting into trouble.

Mike put both hands on his hips, huffed and puffed, and yelled back, "Mom, if you think it's so *damn* easy, you come do it."

I got *the look* from Nancy as soon as the first chuckle came out of me.

About that time, Linda came out of the cabin to investigate. Seeing Caleb and Ethan in the middle of this madhouse of people, dogs, and pigs, she shouted, "Caleb and Ethan, get over here right now." The woman even stamped her foot on the ground.

That made me laugh harder, which unfortunately, proved to be my undoing.

The next thing I know is I had three very ticked off women yelling at me about how my *attitude* was not helping. I couldn't even run away, being that I was still wounded.

My response of continued laughter seemed to egg them on. For a minute or two, I felt like I was back in basic training and being shouted at by Drill Sergeant Ambrose. But in so many ways, this was much worse. Three shouting females breathing down my neck and I couldn't escape…

Eventually, the piglets, one at a time tired out, and were caught. Fortunately, none escaped into the woods, which would have been a bigger problem. Gary made all of the kids get up on the porch when they took the two sows and then the boar out of the wagon. The Winstons had not removed their tusks, so the two animals were rather dangerous.

Hopefully, one on the new piglets was a boar, and we could remedy that with some switching out. Once we had new stock, we'd do the same with the two sows. We just had to be careful. Pigs can be mean, and those tusks were razor sharp.

The existing piglets would be fattened up, and come fall, could become food. The new ones, not yet born, would be the future.

It had felt good to laugh, despite the glares. The memory would be a funny one to bring up for years to come.

***

Rahn entered the hall outside of the administrative offices and quickly looked up and down each hallway. Not seeing who he was looking for, he shouted, "Johnson!"

A few seconds later, Johnson peeked around the corner from an adjoining hallway. "Yeah, First Sergeant?" he said, rubbing his eyes with a fist.

"Get yourself together and meet me at the Hummer," Rahn replied. He spun around and headed for the door.

Now, where is Schwartz?

He pushed the breaker arm on the door as Schwartz burst past him outside. Right behind him was Specialist Johnson, who almost ran into Rahn when he'd stopped and surveyed the other soldiers, who were milling about along with several of the FEMA guards outside.

"Watch where you're going, Johnson," Rahn said lightly. "Come with me." He led Johnson toward their HMWWV, parked under a tree far across the parking lot.

"Where are we going, First Sergeant?" Johnson asked, still groggy, having just been awakened.

"Inside the vehicle," Rahn replied as he walked around to the passenger side and got in.

Johnson entered the drivers side and reached down to start the vehicle.

"Not yet," Rahn said quietly.

"What's up, First Sergeant?" Johnson asked.

"The Major knew just about everything concerning John Henry's fight the other day. The only ones there were you, me, and Schwartz. He could only find out from one of us. I didn't tell him or anyone. So that leaves you and Schwartz. We've been tight, Johnson, but I have to ask. Did you talk to anyone about what happened there?"

"I didn't say anything to anybody, First Sergeant."

Rahn scrutinized Johnson's reaction. The man seemed genuine. "What about Schwartz, did he say anything?"

"I've known him most of my life. He wouldn't say anything, leastwise on purpose?"

"What do you mean, on purpose?"

"Barracks talk, you know. The guys are sitting around, they're bored and telling war stories. He might have said something that way."

"Go find him and bring him here. After that, I need you to grab a few trustworthy guys. The shit just got real, and we have a mission. We aren't coming back from this mission, so quietly grab your personal effects, but only what you can't live without. Hear me?"

Johnson stared at Rahn. "What? What do you mean, not coming back?"

"It's time to bug out, Johnson. The major ordered me to go and arrest John and Brian Henry and bring them back here. He wants their weapons, too. That ain't happening. Not when they need them to defend themselves."

"That would be one serious fight, First Sergeant. Mr. Henry, either one of them, won't obey those orders."

"I know. And I don't blame them. I've made arrangements for them to take us in. I would like to take a few guys with us, people we can trust. Just you and me won't amount to shit. We get a squad, and we might have something."

"I know guys who ain't happy with what's going

on. I can get maybe five or six. Could be a few more. The Henrys don't have enough supplies to take care of all of us, though."

"We'll have to help supply. Get the trailer for this Hummer, and when you get the other guys, get two more Hummers and trailers. Then, we'll go to supply and see if we can draw ammo and other things, steal it if we have to."

"Is that the midnight requisition stuff you talked about when you were back in the old army?"

"I wasn't in the old army, Johnson. I'm in the damn army…" Rahn saw the smirk on Johnson's face and knew instantly the soldier was pulling his chain. "Go get Schwartz first. I need to talk to him. Then, start recruiting other guys for our mission. We don't have a lot of time, and we need to leave in the morning."

"Roger that, First Sergeant," Johnson replied. He hopped out of the HMWWV and took off for the troop area.

Shit. This is getting ready to get ugly. Rahn closed his eyes and thought about everything that had happened, and wondered how Wolfe had learned about the Henrys. He must have dozed off. The rap on the HMWWV door startled him. It was PFC Schwartz and Johnson.

"You wanted to see me, First Sergeant," a nervous-looking Schwartz asked.

Specialist Johnson was almost pressed up against him as he spoke.

Rahn pushed his door slightly open, pointed toward the back, and said to Schwartz, "Get in." Turning to Johnson, he said, "Go do what I told you to do."

"You betchya, First Sergeant."

Rahn just shook his head.

Schwartz got in the back and closed the door. Rahn turned, staring him down. To his credit, Schwartz didn't look away. "I do something wrong, First sergeant?" he asked.

"You tell me," Rahn replied. "I had a rather tense conversation with the major. We talked about the

Henrys. The major knew things, things that only you, Johnson, or me should have known. I know I didn't tell him, and I know Johnson didn't tell him. Guess who rises to the top of the list?"

"I didn't tell him nothin', First Sergeant," Schwartz said. He looked angry.

"What about barracks talk?" Rahn pressed.

Schwartz sat there for a moment, thinking. "Fuck, how could I have been so stupid? I did say something. I'm sorry, First Sergeant."

"Tell me what happened."

"You know how it is, a bunch of us were sittin around talking about what was happening, and what we did in our different sectors. Some of those guys are sick, First Sergeant, I mean real sick in the head. Anyway, I wasn't saying much, and a couple of the guys started raggin' on me about how we weren't doing anything, and how the major was mad about that. So I guess I told them about the fight we saw."

"You guess," Rahn remarked, raising one eyebrow.

"I get it. I used to live in the barracks. I need to trust you, soldier. I need to know that what I tell you, what you see and hear, stays with us. We don't tell anybody anything."

"I understand, First Sergeant. You can believe me."

"I mean anybody, Schwartz, not the major, not Intelligence, not the God damned president of the United States."

"He's dead, First Sergeant," Schwartz said, interrupting Rahn.

"I know. I need you to keep your mouth shut. I don't want you to say anything to anybody, even if they torture you."

"Yes, sir. I've seen that across the road. I don't want anything to do with torture."

"I don't like it, either. Maybe we can change that."

"We're gonna stop them?" Schwartz asked.

"I don't know," Rahn said. He stopped for a minute, thinking carefully about his next words. "Can I trust you, Schwartz?"

"You betchya, First Sergeant," he replied.

What the hell is it with all the 'you betchya's? "Okay, this is what's going down. All your barracks talk got back to the major. He knows what happened with the Henrys, and that includes their Order of Battle."

"What's an Order of Battle?"

"Are you that, oh, never mind. It's weapons and equipment, number of effectives and leadership. That is Order of Battle."

Schwartz nodded his head in understanding.

"The major ordered me, under threat of arrest and court martial, to go round up John and Brian Henry, bring them here under arrest, and confiscate their weapons. He was especially upset about them having automatic weapons and claymores."

"First Sergeant, they won't listen to you. I heard Mr. Henry, the old man that's not in the army. I heard him say he wasn't coming in. You said you wouldn't try and bring him in, either. Have you changed your mind?"

Rahn shook his head. "No, that hasn't changed. I will not try and bring in the Henrys in any more than I'll try to take their weapons."

"So what are you going to do?"

"Join them."

"Can I come, too?" Schwartz asked.

"PFC Schwartz, you don't know how happy it makes me feel to hear you say that."

Schwartz grinned, then got serious. "What do you need me to do, First Sergeant?"

"Johnson is checking with some guys who might want to come along. I want to put a squad together. Who do you know?"

"I can think of a couple men who would be worthy. I can go ask them."

Smiling at the young soldier's enthusiasm, Rahn replied, "No, not yet. What I want you to do is go find Johnson, pull him aside, and quietly tell him who you know. He may have already talked to them. Plus, he knows everything that we need. If he wants you to help him, then do that. If not, go get your gear and don't let anyone know why."

"You betchya, First Sergeant."

"Schwartz?"

"Yes."

"Do you reply to a military directive by saying you betchya?"

"No, First Sergeant."

"Just how do you respond?"

"With roger, First Sergeant."

"Then do it, PFC."

"Hooah," Schwartz said, enthusiasm thick in his reply. He opened the vehicle door, got out, and took off in the direction of the barracks.

Privates. Rahn thought as he leaned back in the vehicle seat, tipped his hat over his eyes, and decided he needed to finish his nap. He might not get a chance to do so for a while.

***

The excitement with the pigs turned into a godsend. The energy used and the laughter had released a lot of tension in all of us. It was the stress that we had all been carrying around for months, and in one crazy afternoon, it all disappeared. Supper that night, communal-style again, was an enjoyable time. Almost like none of the last several months had ever happened. We felt like one huge happy family.

After dinner, I snagged a cup of coffee from the top of the stove. It smelled burnt, having been there most of the day. I mostly just wanted to hold it. What I really needed was a cigar, but I had been asked not to smoke in front of the kids. Specifically, not in front of Linda's kids. She was afraid it might make them sick.

That was about the silliest thing I had ever heard, and I was surprised that I gave in so easily. A couple of the others had remarked the same.

The truth was I liked Linda. I still missed Carol a lot, but Linda helped fill a void. She had spunk, and was definitely a survivor. She raised her boys right, too. She wasn't afraid to let them get dirty, and I even heard her tell the oldest one that he should have listened to her or he wouldn't have hurt himself. That kind of parenting is long gone, or I thought it was. It made me feel good to see that.

I was back in my chair, sitting on only one pillow now. I might keep using a pillow; it felt good on these old bones. The carrying on inside the house sounded good. The creak of the screen door—Sam had offered to fix it—caused me to look up. It was Brian. He was holding a glass of something. It was getting dark, and I couldn't tell what it was. His big hands covered most of the glass anyway.

"Howdy, Pops," he said as he went to the chair furthest away from me. That made me suspicious.

"Howdy, son," I replied, keeping my eyes on him.

He grinned, took a sip from his glass, and leaned back in the homemade Adirondack style chair. I had made four chairs years ago from some plans my dad had. The one with the space for a cup holder and ashtray in the arms was mine. The others didn't have that refinement.

He took another sip and made an "aaaaah" sound. He was up to something.

Then, just like that, it hit me. Some years ago, I had found a bottle of Rebel Yell Whiskey on the internet. Wisconsin is one of those states you can get mail-order liquor in, and I ordered some. I actually ordered a case. It's a high-grade whiskey generally only sold south of the Mason-Dixon line. That is, in part, why they call it Rebel Yell.

"That my whiskey?" I asked rather firmly.

"Yup."

"Did you ask?"

"Pops, you said *mi casa es su casa*."

"I did *not* say that."

"Yes, you did."

I glared at him. "I don't speak Spanish. Why are you drinking my whiskey?"

"You said we were to treat ourselves as if this was our home. That we could have anything we wanted *except* your cigars."

"You took some of my cigars."

"I forgot your rule."

"You've obviously forgotten another."

He glanced at me. "You didn't say I couldn't."

"Fine, enjoy the damn whiskey. Next time, ask."

"I didn't mean to make you upset, Dad."

Then, as Brian used to do when he was a kid—and always the little con artist—he snickered.

That made me laugh. We were both losing our minds over something as dumb as stealing whiskey. It felt good.

"Oh, shit!" Brian exclaimed.

"What?" Swiveling my head around, I tried to see if anything was wrong.

"I almost spilled."

"Gimme the glass, Brian. You can't be trusted. Spilling is a sin."

He took a final sip, the glass still about three-quarters full, and gave it to me. "I'm going to bed." Leaning over, he kissed me on top of my head. "G'night Pops. You can smoke your cigar now." And with a laugh, he went inside.

I listened to my son's advice. I went through the ritual of cutting and lighting my cigar, the one I had hidden from everyone until they had all gone to bed, then took a sip of my whiskey.

There was no way I was going to drink the whole glass. I had no idea what he was thinking when he poured such a large amount. I figured I'd drink a bit of it, cover it up, and save the rest for later after I hid my remaining bottles. I'd keep one out for all the adults to enjoy one night on a special occasion. I wasn't completely selfish.

Leaning back in my chair and closing my eyes, I was enjoying the quiet. All of the night critters were chirping, making for an excellent musical accompaniment to the night.

Then I heard the door creak. "No, you can't have any more whiskey, Brian. You're cut off," I said.

"It's Linda, and I don't drink straight whiskey. There's that old saying."

Sitting up, I asked, "What old saying?"

"Whiskey makes you frisky."

I chuckled. "Well, I certainly wasn't…"

She laughed and said, "No, I wasn't thinking that." She came over and sat in the chair next to me, holding her hand out and silently asking for the glass.

"I thought you didn't drink whiskey?"

"Sometimes, you have to break the rules, and I think I need a sip."

"Rough day?"

"No, all the excitement took care of that. I'm just feeling mellow, and this seemed like a nice place to treat that. I noticed no one has any dark chocolate, which is what I am dying for."

"I may have some stashed away." I started to get up, but she reached over and put her hand on my arm. "Save it for later, John."

I realized I still had the cigar in my hand, and I don't know why, but I asked her if I should put it out.

"No, your cigars actually smell good. Most people I knew that smoked didn't smoke cigars that smell that good."

"It's quality tobacco. I thought that because you had asked me not to smoke around the boys…"

"That's for them. I like the smell of a good cigar. Back home, I had a very close friend who smoked them. He called them premium cigars. My company helped move him somewhere that he could continue to enjoy them. Seems where he lived didn't allow any smoking, even outside."

"That should be against the law," I remarked.

"He would agree. I wonder where he is now. Nice guy, even made wine in an Instant Pot."

"That doesn't sound good."

"It wasn't too bad. I just prefer fruity wines and those take longer."

"We have a lot of fruit around here—berries, apples, grapes, and I think some pears, too at one of the neighboring places. I have recipes. Maybe we could try and make some."

"I might enjoy that, if it can be done."

"Oh ye of little faith," I commented and took an exaggerated puff on my cigar.

"I see why you like it out here on the porch," she said, changing the subject.

"It's quiet. I do a lot of thinking out here. The porch has become something of a sanctuary for me as much as a symbol."

"A symbol for what?"

"For all of us here. When we're on the porch, it becomes our world, like all those worlds up there," I explained, pointing to the sky. The natural darkness here with no light from anywhere made the stars brilliant this night. "Each of those stars are their own little world, like in that Robert Browning poem where he writes, "'What matter to me if their star is a world? Mine has opened its soul to me; therefore, I love it.'"

"Sorry, I'm not into poetry."

I shrugged. "It was a poem that got me to move here. One by Yeats. "'I will arise and go now, and go to Innisfree, And a small cabin build there.'"

She laughed. "This isn't exactly what I'd call a *small* cabin, John. Are you some kind of professor?"

"No, I just read a lot. Or used to anyway." No one had ever called me a professor before, and I wasn't certain how I felt about it.

"Anyway," she said, "I really came out here to talk to you."

"About what?" I asked, giving her my full attention.

"I wanted to say…thank you."

"For what?"

"For letting us stay here. I had nowhere to go, and after finding out about my aunt and uncle, I probably would have ended up in one of those camps with my boys that you guys talk about. I'm glad I didn't. When I first met you, I thought you were a grouch.

Donna even said you could be sometimes."

"She would," I said, rather snarkily. "She's my ex-wife for a reason."

"Anyway, you aren't. You're a good man, John Henry. A very good man." She held her hand out for the glass again, and I handed it to her.

Taking another sip, she stood up, leaned over, and gave me a warm hug. Then, she went inside. It was a nice hug.

Chapter 12

*"Dangerous journeys require the same number of
steps as safe ones. The only difference is the amount
of perspiration."*

—Chris Rahn

R ahn awoke with a stiff back and neck. *I shoulda
went to bed in my quarters.* Still in the HMWWV,
he sat there for a moment. Then, he got out of the
vehicle and went to his quarters. Grabbing his duffle
bag and backpack, he filled them with clothes he knew
he would need, including his winter gear and personal
items. Taking them back to the HMWWV, he threw
them in the back and went inside to the admin area to
get some requisition forms.

Finding what he was looking for, he completed the
form for ammo, weapons, explosives, and MREs.
Completing the forms, he forged Wolfe's signature to
them and went back out to the HMWWV. Specialist
Johnson should be arriving soon, and they would have
to be at the requisition point early—before Wolfe
came into the office at 9 AM, his usual time.

Johnson arrived about 30 minutes later. He and
Schwartz had nine soldiers with them in three
HMWWVs. That gave them four with trailers. If they
could pull this off, they'd be alright.

Each of the soldiers had their basic weapon, with
six 30 round magazines each. Two of the vehicles had
SAWS, which gave them a total of four when counting

162

the one the Henrys had. The SAW gunners each had an M9 sidearm.

What I'd give for a couple M224 Light Mortars, but I've had zero chance of getting any. I'm not even certain we have any in the camp.

"Okay, people, gather round," Rahn ordered.

The soldiers loosely circled around him.

"We'll talk more later. Right now, I want everyone to think hard about what we are doing. We need to go to the requisition point to fill these requisitions."

Holding them up in his hand, he briefly told the men what was on the list. "If anyone asks, we are heading out on a combat mission to engage and seize a rebellious force, arrest it's members, confiscate their weapons and return here. That is all you know. Questions?"

The men stood silently; no questions were raised.

"Okay, mount up, and let's head out. Follow me and Johnson."

All of the soldiers entered their vehicles and followed Rahn to the requisition point. A lone guard stood at its entrance, concertina wire on an X frame blocked the entry. The guard held his hand up for them to stop, and the small convoy came to a halt. Rahn got out of the vehicle and approached the guard.

"We're here to fill this and head out," he told the guard.

"There's just a duty soldier in there now, Top," the guard said.

"Don't call me Top, soldier. I'm a First Sergeant. We had this set up yesterday. I'm taking this force out on a mission, and we need to get an early start. Call the duty soldier."

"Yes, First Sergeant," the guard replied as he went to a field phone resting on a stack of sandbags. Finishing his call, he came back.

"The duty guy wasn't sure he should, but I told him you had all the forms and were a First Sergeant. He said he'd try to fill it for you."

"So, it's not ready?" Rahn said gruffly.

"I'm guessing not, First Sergeant. Typical army screw up, but Specialist Prine, that's his name, he said he'd square you away."

"Thank you, soldier," Rahn said and returned to the HMWWV.

The guard pulled back the X Frame and waved the convoy in. Johnson led them to a row of CONEX containers and stopped. A soldier stood there waiting for them.

Rahn got out and approached the soldier with the requisitions. Shining his flashlight on the order, the soldier looked it over. "This is a lot of stuff, First Sergeant."

"We're expecting trouble, Specialist, so we're going prepared."

"I might not have everything," he said.

"Give us what we can, and we'll be on our way," Rahn said. "My soldiers can help load."

"No problem, First Sergeant." And the loading began.

They finished as the sun was coming up. Rahn looked at his watch. The time was 0745. *Perfect.*

He signed the forms, thanked the Specialist, and the convoy headed out. Taking Stewart Avenue toward Highway 51, they made their way toward the Henrys.

They took Highway 51 south until they reached Highway 29, going east. Crossing the Wisconsin River, Rahn directed Johnson to lead them forward, heading through Schofield and on to Wittenberg. From Wittenberg, they would go north until they reached Lake View.

"Some of the guys grabbed some extra ammo and grenades. Claymores, too," Johnson remarked as he cruised down the trafficless road.

"I would have thought less of them had they not, Johnson," Rahn said casually.

"I told them that, First Sergeant."

On the outskirts of Weston, Rahn had Johnson take an off-ramp and then pull over where he could talk with the new team more freely. Everyone exited their vehicles and gathered around him.

"I know Specialist Johnson told you what we were doing, but I wanted you to hear it from me. First, if anyone has second thoughts, now is the time to pull out. You're free to go if that's what you want." Rahn stood there looking at each man in the eye individually, trying to sense doubt or a change of mind.

"We're all in, First Sergeant," one of the soldiers said. "We don't like what's happening, and Johnson told us the score. Somebody has to stand up to these people. Guess it's gonna be us and this family we're going to help."

"This family," Rahn began, "is the Henry family. Mr. John Henry is a retired Army Master Sergeant. His son, Mr. Brian Henry, is a Chief Warrant Officer 2 in the regular U.S. Army. Technically, he just became your commanding officer. There are young women in this group, two of them. You will leave them alone. I hear any shit, and somebody will be in serious trouble. There are families, kids, a former marine, and a sailor. These people won't put up with any garbage. You screw up out there, and someone will put you in the ground. They are good people, but they won't put up with trouble." He paused for a moment to let his words sink in. "So, I'll ask you again; anyone want to back out?"

No one spoke up.

"So, here's the situation," Rahn continued. "We're going there to start a new life. We will work. That means normal army stuff like guard duty and patrols. It also means farming and building quarters. The Henrys aren't expecting this many people, so we'll have to build cabins before the snow flies. You'll also get to hunt and fish, but that's for subsistence, not recreation."

"First Sergeant, I don't have a hunting or fishing license," one of the soldiers said.

"I don't think that matters anymore, soldier," Rahn said as some of the others chuckled. "Any questions?"

When it was obvious there were none, Rahn said,

"Saddle up, people, let's go to Lake View."

The men loaded up into their vehicles, and the convoy headed down the road.

***

Wolfe finished his breakfast in the dining hall and went to his office. He was there about 15 minutes when the Supply Sergeant from the requisition point came to his door and knocked.

"Enter," he barked at the door.

A large, slightly round man wearing ACUs walked into the office. "Major Wolfe, I'm Staff Sergeant Brandon, the Requisition Property Non-Commissioned Officer in Charge."

"What is it, Staff Sergeant? I'm pretty busy," Wolfe answered.

"Sir, I have some requisitions here that seem a bit, um, excessive for a patrol. Your signature is on them as authorizing them."

Not looking up from the paperwork he was reviewing, Wolfe said, "Bring them here, Staff Sergeant," and holding his hand out to receive them.

The sergeant walked across the room and placed a manila folder in Wolfe's outstretched hand.

Wolfe set the folder down on his desk and continued to work on the documents in front of him. The Staff Sergeant stood patiently, his hands resting in the small of his back, his uniform blouse stretched tight against his body. After a few minutes, Wolfe finished and turned his attention to the folder the Staff Sergeant had given him.

"Let's see what you have here," Wolfe remarked as he opened the folder. Removing the documents, he set the folder down and began to read through them. "This does seem excessive. When did you receive these?"

"Sir, my Duty Soldier filled that requisition early this morning."

"This morning? So what's the problem, Staff Sergeant?"

"Sir, we always ask for 24-hours advanced notice of requisitions of this size, and generally, no one is to pick up an order before oh nine hundred."

Major Wolfe continued to look through the documents. Coming to the last page, he saw the authorizing signature over his typed name, rank, and position. "Staff Sergeant, this is not my signature. This document is a forgery."

"Damn, I was afraid of that, Sir."

"Who picked up the requisition? Who signed for it?"

"Major, there is another document in the folder; it's a receipt of the requisition. It is signed by a First Sergeant Chris Rahn."

"Say that name again," Wolfe said as he picked up the folder and withdrew the receipt. There, on the bottom of the form, as a signature and printed name, Chris Rahn, First Sergeant.

Wolfe abruptly stood up, grabbed the papers, and bolted from the room.

As he passed the Staff Sergeant, he said, "Wait here, I'll be right back."

Wolfe headed down the hall to a room almost at the very end. On entering the room, one immediately noticed several large maps on repurposed rolling chalkboards along the walls in front of the windows were banks of olive drab colored radios. In front of each sat an operator. Rushing to the first one he could reach, he ordered, "Soldier, I need you to contact First Sergeant Rahn."

"His operator or him personally, sir," the operator asked.

"I want him on that radio right now, soldier!" Wolfe loudly ordered.

The entire room grew very silent, and the radio operator picked up the handset, keyed it, and spoke into it. "Antigo 7 Actual, Antigo 7 Actual, this is Antigo 6, over." Releasing the key, he waited.

No reply came.

Trying again, the radio operator said, "Antigo 7 Actual, Antigo 7 Actual, this is Antigo 6, over."

Still, nothing was returned.

"Again, soldier," Wolfe ordered.

"Antigo 7 Actual, Antigo 7 Actual, this is Antigo 6, over." Still, no reply. "Nothing, sir," the operator said.

"You keep trying. I If you get him, order him to return here immediately. You tell him that is a direct order from me, do you understand?"

"Yes, Sir."

Wolfe left the room and headed back toward his office. Instead of entering, he went to the Regional FEMA Administrators office, and without knocking, walked through the open door.

"Richard, we may have a problem," Wolfe announced as he walked up to the thin, balding man with round plastic frame glasses, small beady eyes, and a pencil-thin moustache.

"What kind of problem, Elias?" the administrator asked in a high-pitched male voice.

Major Wolfe showed the requisition forms to him, explaining what some of the items were and then showed him where Rahn had signed for the equipment. He then explained the conversation he had yesterday with Rahn about the Henrys and how he was concerned that Rahn might have turned.

"Where is Rahn now?" Richard asked.

"I have the Communications Center trying to contact him now."

"If he's turned and run, Elias, he isn't going to answer that radio."

"I suppose you're right. I have the Com Center trying anyway."

"Get Captain Jamison and have him assemble the Quick Reaction Force."

"I can get my soldiers to go after him. This is what they've trained for," Wolfe said.

"I highly doubt your men are going to chase down their First Sergeant and either arrest him or shoot him."

"They'll do their duty. They're soldiers."

"Like Rahn," Richard said as he sat down behind

his desk. "I have high hopes for you, Elias. This will not look good for you if it doesn't get fixed. Did he take anyone with him?"

"He probably took his driver and another private. The three of them were always together," Wolfe said.

"Well, you better find out. I remember years ago when I was in the army. I was discharged in basic training for bad eyes, you know. When I was in the army, a First Sergeant was like a God. Your soldiers may be more loyal to him, and as a result, a bigger problem. You need to find out, Elias."

Richard sat down and began to look through papers on his desk, signaling the meeting was over. As Wolfe was heading out the door, Richard said, "Don't forget to tell Captain Jamison to assemble the Quick Reaction Force. I want them on the road in 15 minutes. Have him report to me before he heads out."

Wolfe turned, dropped his head, and walked out of the Administrator's Office.

***

"Antigo 7 Actual, Antigo 7 Actual, this is Antigo 6, over," the voice came over the speaker box inside the HMWWV. They were now north of Wittenberg, heading up Highway 45 past the former Ho-Chunk Casino.

"Should I get that, First Sergeant?" Johnson asked.

"Nope. That's Wolfe, and he probably just learned of our requisition," Rahn said.

"Roger that," replied Johnson.

"Antigo 7 Actual, Antigo 7 Actual, this is Antigo 6, over," came the call again and again.

"Sounds like he really wants to talk to you, First Sergeant."

"Pull over, Johnson," Rahn said abruptly.

Johnson gave Rahn a sideways glance before he pulled the vehicle over to the side of the road. The others pulled in behind them.

"Call everybody up here," Rahn said, as he got out of the vehicle, went over to some low bushes on the side of the road, and relieved himself. When he finished and buttoned his pants, he went to the assembled group.

"Men, I know everybody heard those radio calls. That's Major Wolfe looking for us. Mostly me, but looking for all of us. No one, and I mean *no one*, will contact them, answer them, or reply to them in any way. Got it?"

"Got it," they all replied.

"Cat's out of the bag, gentlemen. They know we're gone. They may not yet know who you are, but they will soon. There is no turning back for any of us now."

"HOOAH!" the men shouted.

Twirling his index finger in the air, Rahn said, "Okay men, mount up. Let's go to our new home."

***

Sam Karpinski was in the new radio room of the first dogtrot cabin they had built. He had been listening in on a variety of transmissions, some from as far away as Florida. Dialing through the frequencies, he heard, "Antigo 7 Actual, Antigo 7 Actual, this is Antigo 6, over."

Pausing, because he recognized Rahn's call-sign, he heard it again. "Antigo 7 Actual, Antigo 7 Actual, this is Antigo 6, over."

"Something's up," he said.

He started to begin his radio shut down procedure when he again heard, "Antigo 7 Actual, Antigo 7 Actual, this is Antigo 6, over."

Turning the HAM radio off, he left the cabin and headed over to what they were now calling The Big House. John didn't think it was funny, but everyone else did.

John was in the back, checking out the tomatoes. They were still big and green, but some had a hint of ripening color starting to show.

John saw Sam heading his way. "Won't be long, Sam, won't be long, and we'll have more tomatoes than we know what to do with."

"Fresh tomatoes are always good. John, the radio messages I've been picking up may not be good," Sam said, kneeling down, getting a closer look at the produce.

John straightened, giving him his full attention. "What messages?"

Sam stood. "Seems our friend Rahn is missing. His headquarters is looking for him, and he hasn't answered the call."

"Hmmm. Maybe he's out of range, or we can't hear his response?" John suggested.

"It's possible but doubtful. I've picked up communications in Florida."

"So he's out of their range. You know how wonky those vehicular mounted radios can be."

"Possible, but it could also mean trouble. Rahn got ambushed or…" Sam stopped before stating what he feared.

"You know he didn't get ambushed, and if he did, it would be a serious problem. It could be something else," John said.

"You think he was sent out to get you like he said would happen? Maybe he decided to hell with it and is now going over the hill."

"I'm more inclined to believe that. Last time I talked with him, he said Wolfe was telling him to bring me in. I told him we weren't coming, and he said he knew that. Said flat out, he wouldn't even try."

"I kinda figured that. He seems honorable. I trust him," Sam said.

"Well, if it's trouble, he'll show up here. You can count on that. It's going to happen, and we have the third cabin for him. I suspect Specialist Johnson will come with him, too. We should probably make sure those wood stoves work. Won't be long and they'll be needed."

"I'll get one of the guys to help me. I'll test 'em out.

I'm gonna need a working stove, too. We can't all live in the Big House ya' know."

"You know I don't like that Big House talk. This isn't a plantation, and those aren't slave quarters."

"I'm just teasing, John. You know that."

"Teasing is fine, but that's just plain mean, Sam," John replied. "Take, Allen, Sam. He's out of bed and has been looking for something to do. Shouldn't be too strenuous, and it will help him feel like he's doing something useful."

"Will do. Save me some tomatoes. I don't want to find out you've been eating them and not sharing. That would hurt my feelings."

"You're a sailor, Sam. You don't have feelings."

Both men chuckled.

***

Rahn's convoy approached Lake View. They drove past Carol's house, and Rahn noticed buzzards circling the field.

"Turn here, Johnson," he directed. "Buzzards shouldn't be circling around. They might have missed somebody."

Johnson turned the wheel sharply to the right, sending Rahn banging into the door and almost upsetting the trailer.

"HEY!" Schwartz yelled from the turret. "Let a guy know before you do that."

"Sorry," Johnson said with a hint of not really in his voice. "Boy needs to learn how to pay attention, First Sergeant," Johnson said.

"That apply to me, too, Specialist," Rahn replied without amusement as he rubbed his shoulder.

"You told me to turn," Johnson said defensively. "I was just following orders."

"People have been hung for *just* following orders, Johnson."

"Yes, First Sergeant."

The small convoy bounced through Carol's yard and entered the field. The wreckage of motorcycles was still there.

Rahn told Johnson to stop. He stepped out of the HMWWV and signaled for everyone else to do the same. "Schwartz, stay up there and keep your eyes peeled. I don't want any surprises."

"Yes, First Sergeant," Schwartz replied and began slowly turning in a circle, checking out the terrain and its perimeter.

The others joined Rahn. One of them remarked, "Is this where Schwartz's battle happened?"

"Yeah, it wasn't really much of a battle. The Henrys have been lucky so far. They've had vastly superior firepower, and their antagonists have had what amounts to little more than peashooters," Rahn said.

"Damn waste of good bikes," another soldier commented. "I'd love to have one. Those are all Harleys."

"Well, they don't look like they work anymore," one of the other soldiers said.

"First Sergeant," a tall blonde one said, getting Rahn's attention. "We could make one or two of these cycles operational. Cannibalize the others for parts. Be good for scouting instead of using these gas hog Hummers. At least until we run out of petrol and have to walk again."

"We're grunts," another responded. "We walk, and then we get the shitty end of the stick."

"What's your name, soldier?" Rahn asked.

"Me, First Sergeant?" the one who had made the suggestion asked. "Bennet, PFC Michael Bennet."

"Well, PFC Bennet, that's an outstanding idea. After we get set up at the Henrys, bring a couple of guys out here, pick up whatever you need from this wreckage, and take it back in the trailer. I hear these things get good gas mileage, and they'd be like gasoline-powered horses."

"Roger that, First Sergeant," Bennet said as he puffed up his chest and strutted around.

Rahn watched him out of the corner of his eye. *It was a good idea, and these guys needed encouragement. This is a good win.*

"Anybody see what's drawing the buzzards?" Rahn asked.

The men spread out and began to search the area.

"Feels like I'm on a police call," a private named Owens said. "I ain't policing nothing up off the ground."

"You will if the First Sergeant tells you to," Specialist Bob Hart said.

"Yes, Specialist," Owens replied.

"FIRST SERGEANT," Hart called out. "I think I found it."

Rahn walked over to see what it was. On the ground in front of him was a sizeable coagulating pile of blood. It reeked, too.

"Could be?" Rahn said. "Anybody else see anything?"

A chorus of "No, First Sergeant" came back.

"Okay, mount up. Let's get to the Henrys," he announced.

The men all climbed into their vehicles, and with Johnson leading, drove toward the Henrys' cabin.

***

Sajan was in the bunker when he heard the vehicles coming down the road. Taking a quick glance in that direction, he slipped back inside the bunker and grabbed the field phone, vigorously cranking the handle on its side.

"Hello," Addie answered as she was closest to the phone in the cabin.

"We got company, a lot of company. Looks like the army," Sajan explained.

He waited, his weapon at the ready, and kept alert as the vehicles got closer.

***

"Okay, thanks for the heads up." Addie set the phone down and called out through the back door. "John, Sajan called. Looks like the army is coming," she shouted.

She grabbed her AR. *Never a dull moment around here.*

***

I waved at Addie, acknowledging her message, and began the trek toward the cabin. I didn't get very far before I saw four HMWWVs pulling up, each towing a trailer. *What the hell?*

They all stopped, and I recognized Rahn and Johnson in the front seat of the lead vehicle. Waving at him, I headed their way.

"What's up, and what is all of this?" I asked, waving my hands at the entourage.

"Big trouble, John," Rahn replied. "You got a minute? Let's sit down and talk." He glanced at the HMWWVs. "Where would you like my guys to put all of this equipment?"

John gestured toward the barn. "Have them put it in the barn. You can use one of the stalls, for now. The horses are in the paddocks."

"Johnson!" Rahn yelled.

"Yes, First Sergeant," Johnson said.

"Unload all of this gear in the barn, put the stuff in one of the stalls. Then, everyone can break in place until we figure the rest out," Rahn said.

Specialist Johnson put everyone to work, and Rahn and I walked to the porch to sit down. "So, what's the big trouble?" I asked.

"I got ordered under threat of court-martial to bring you and the chief in, plus confiscate your weapons."

"That explains the radio calls that Sam heard."

"You heard those, huh?"

"Yeah. So how many men did you bring with you?" I asked.

"Counting me, Johnson and Schwartz, I brought a total of twelve men. We'll need them."

"It gives us a better force, that's for sure. We'll need to build another cabin or two, depending on how you want to bunk 'em. Gonna have to find a couple more stoves, too. I assume they're trustworthy? Won't be heading back to report to Wolfe?"

"They are, and happy to have a home. Won't be long before it's cold, and no offense, but I don't want to sleep in the barn or a GP large, even if I had a GP large. I can send some guys out to search for the stoves, no problem."

"Good. We've got cabin building down to an art. With the extra manpower, we can build two more in just a couple of days," I said.

"Just tell 'em what to do, and they'll do it. I don't know them all that well, but Johnson and Schwartz do."

Brian came out on the porch. He looked like he'd just woke up as he had a bad case of bed head.

"Hey, First Sergeant," he mumbled.

"Hello, Chief, brought you some troops."

"Huh?" Brian asked, scanning the yard.

"You have a command now, Chief," Rahn said, "and I need you to get them ready because Wolfe will be coming soon, that I can assure you."

"Why? What's going on?" Brian asked, stifling a yawn as he sat down next to us. "Sorry, I had guard last night."

"Like I was telling John, I got ordered to come and get the two of you, confiscate your weapons and bring you back, under arrest if necessary."

"That shit ain't happening," Brian said.

"Brian, just listen," I said, glancing from Rahn to my son.

Rahn looked at Brian. "That's why I'm here. Wolfe started using words like treason."

"Is he nuts?" Brian asked.

Rahn shrugged. "More like drunk with power. Him and the FEMA administrator have a regular concentration camp going. Some of the stories I've heard will turn your stomach."

Brian raised an eyebrow. "What kind of stories?"

"Summary executions, slave labor, abuse of female prisoners. That kind of shit."

"Sorry I asked," Brian replied.

"From what Sam has picked up on his HAM," I said, "that's going on in other parts of the country, too. Corruption seems to be a new industry."

"So, how big is my command?" Brian said with a slight hint of sarcasm.

"Twelve, counting me. I'm your first sergeant."

"No shit?" Brian replied, his grin returned.

"No shit, Chief. A whole reinforced squad."

"Welcome back to the army, son," I said jovially.

"We'll need to get 'em billeted, fixed up for weapons, and so on," Brian said absently.

"I brought stuff, a lot of stuff," Rahn said.

"Oh?" Brian asked, scanning the yard again.

"Yes, Sir. Four hummers with four full trailers. We brought two more SAWS, three counting mine, cases of 5.56, grenades, 9 mm, claymores, and a lot of other stuff."

"Any indirect fire?"

"I wish. I don't think there is any available, and if so, it isn't up here."

"Good job, First Sergeant. I guess I need to meet the troops then. How do I look?"

"You need a haircut," Rahn answered.

"Screw you, Top. Let's go meet the troops."

I chuckled as I watched my son and First Sergeant walk away, and got a glare for my reaction from Brian. That didn't stop me from wondering what would be in store for all of us in the days to come.

Chapter 13

"When you're running down traitors, the chase is almost as good as the end result."

—Roy Jamison

Captain Roy Jamison, Commander of the FEMA Quick Reaction Force, was a tall, sandy-haired man of medium build. His all-black uniform projected authority and a certain sense of intimidation. He joined Major Elias Wolfe in the FEMA Regional Administrator's office of Richard Barstow.

"Roy, I want you to take the QRF and find Rahn. Bring him back, dead or alive. I don't care how, but I want that son of a bitch back here. All the equipment he took, too," Richard Barstow said.

"No problem, Richard. But I think we need to slow down a little," Roy replied.

"Why?" Richard asked.

"We don't know exactly where he is, other than somewhere east of Antigo."

"There's more, Richard," Wolfe interjected.

"What more, Elias?"

"He has several men with him."

"I'm just now finding this out? You disappoint me, Elias. How many?"

Elias startled. "A dozen are missing. I just found out myself, Richard."

"All the more reason to go slow," Roy said. "We take a team north, and then I suggest we send out two scout teams. They can find them, call the rest of us, and we'll get him. We'll bivouac at the armory in Antigo."

"Good plan. I want that son of a bitch!" Richard exploded.

"I'd like to go with him, Richard. I know the area. They are most likely in Lake View somewhere." Wolfe said.

"That's a damn good idea. If you don't find them, maybe you'll stay up there and get shot, cuz I'm mad enough to have you shot!" Richard yelled.

"Richard, I'm sorry…" Wolfe gulped.

Richard slammed his fist on the desk. "Sorry don't cut it anymore, Elias. Find him, or you'll not be in your lofty role anymore, understand?"

"Yes, Sir," Wolfe replied.

"That's more like it. Okay, Roy, take this…this Wolfe with you, and get set up in Antigo. Let me know when you get there."

"Will do," Roy answered.

***

Brian and Rahn walked over to the group of soldiers, who were standing around near the barn. Rahn shouted, "Specialist Johnson, get these men into formation. Two squads."

"Yes, First Sergeant," Johnson replied.

"Hart, take the second squad. I'll take the first. Okay, men, FALL IN!" Johnson said as he took charge of the group.

The men quickly got into two squads, performed a dress right dress maneuver to ensure the proper interval by extending their right arms out and touching the shoulder of the man to their right.

The second squad then centered themselves on the man in front of them and came to the military position of Attention.

First Sergeant Rahn took a position immediately in

front of and centered on the two squads and also stood at Attention. He executed an About Face, saluted, and said, "Sir, the Command is formed."

Brian, a little taken aback and trying not to smile, walked forward, stood in front of the First Sergeant, saluted, and whispered, "It's a bit much, isn't it, Rahn?"

"It's important, Chief. They need this."

Brian whispered again, "Okay, then." He gave the order, "Post."

First Sergeant Rahn turned and walked behind the formation.

Brian then gave the command, "At Ease," which allowed the soldiers to stand in place in a more relaxed pose, but not talk as they waited for his next words.

"I'm Chief Warrant Officer Two, Brian Henry. I am now your commanding officer. I have to tell you; things may be a bit more casual around here than you may be used to. We also have to remember, we are *soldiers*, and we have to conduct ourselves as *soldiers*. Now, I don't know you, and you don't know me. So starting with you, Specialist Johnson, tell me who you are and your rank."

"Sir, I'm Specialist Felix Johnson," Johnson said.

A few snickers were heard from the group.

"At ease," Rahn commanded softly.

The man next to Johnson went next and introduced himself. "Sir, I'm PFC Jay Schwartz."

In turn, each man identified himself. They were Specialist Danny Myer, PFC Dale Klotz, Private Bill Owens, Specialist Rob Jones, Specialist Bob Hart, PFC Michael Bennet, PFC Chuck Travis, Specialist Richard Klause, and Private William Roop.

"Good to meet each of you," Brian said. "I see no reason at this time to change the squads, so stay where you are. For now, we need to get you bunked in, fed, and introduce you to the others here in our little group. There are fifteen of us, counting me; we also have three kids and two dogs. Our overall leader is my dad, John Henry, who is retired U.S. Army. We have a former marine and sailor amongst us."

Brian paced in front of the group. "The sailor, Sam Karpinski, operates our HAM radio. He lets us know how bad the world has gone to shit. We have two guard points, one in the front by the road and another out in the back near the garden, facing the tree line across the field."

He paused, giving thought to what he should say next. "We weren't expecting you so soon, so you may have to enjoy those MREs the First Sergeant told me that you borrowed."

Light laughter came from the group.

"Most of you will, for now, bunk in the barn. We only have one extra cabin. Tomorrow, you will be assigned to a variety of details, some of which will be building two more cabins. We don't have materials for more than two cabins right now, so living in the barn will be your home until we get those cabins built." Brian paused again. "My dad is old army, and he tells me that in the old army, they took better care of their horses than they did the soldiers. So, the barn should be pretty comfortable for you. He should know. He rode horses for the army."

"Aw c'mon, Chief, ain't nobody rode horses in the army for a hundred years," one of the soldiers in the last row commented.

"Well, guess what soldier, he did. He was in The Old Guard and rode those horses while burying soldiers in Arlington."

"No shit," PFC Klotz said. "That's a strac unit."

"No shit," Brian replied. "So take the rest of the day, relax, check your gear, and keep your combat loads handy. We have had problems out here, and we all know that they are going to come looking for you. You have the rest of the day off."

That brought several hooahs from the group.

"First Sergeant," Brain shouted.

Rahn came to the front of the formation and stood in front of Brian. "They are all yours. Get 'em squared away and then come see me. We need to talk."

***

Elias Wolfe and Captain Roy Jamison and their twenty-five man QRF team pulled into the Antigo Armory parking lot that evening. The eight black HMWWVs backed into the parking spots in such a way that they could leave quickly, if need be. Surprisingly, a tank still stood untouched in front of the one-story red brick building. Although, how anyone could steal it was another thing.

The building itself was a different story. It had been broken into, obviously by people looking for food, weapons, or anything else of use. Someone, or actually several someones, had used one of the offices for a bathroom.

Pigs. Major Wolfe wandered down the hall toward what had been his office. As he entered it, he saw the room had been turned into a trash heap. The desk had been overturned, all the drawers pulled out, and their contents scattered over the floor.

He began to straighten things by first uprighting the desk and returning the drawers to their proper place. As he was putting things away, Roy Jamison came in.

"Quite a mess, isn't it, Elias?" he stated matter-of-factly.

"Yeah, they trashed things pretty badly. We should send out patrols and find anyone still in town. Maybe bring them back here and make them clean this up."

Roy laughed. "That's not what we're here for. We don't have time to seek retribution because the armory was a recreation area for everyone in town with a grudge against the government."

"That's too bad. A little revenge right now would feel good," Elias said.

"All your CONEXs in the back have been broken into. Nothing is left in them."

"Wasn't much of value. Just some tents, field stoves, stuff like that. All the weapons and ammo we took with us to Wausau."

"That's good. We don't need a heavily armed insurgency here in town, bad enough we have one at Henry's. Speaking of, I'm sending two parties out to drive around there, see what they can find."

"I should go with them," Elias said.

"Not yet. You'll get your chance," Roy responded. "I want to let those people know we are here, even if we don't see them."

"Which way did you send the scouts?" Elias asked, changing the subject.

"Straight out Highway 64 toward Lake View. It's a major road. They'll be seen, and that's exactly what I want to happen. If they make contact, I told them not to engage. I want them to drive through that town, head out to the park east of town and then come back. That's the general area they are in, according to your reports of that looter band they wiped out."

"Yep, they're in that general area. No doubt they'll be seen."

"You'll get your chance soon, Wolfe."

***

Fred and Billy Winston rode home after having spent the day hunting turkey. There was no shortage of them around their place, but they didn't want to spook the birds and not have them around come winter. Instead, they took the horses and rode a few miles away to go wild turkey hunting. Ever since the EMP, the turkey population appeared to be growing and the birds were less afraid of people.

They each had two turkeys draped across their saddles. As they crested a small rise in the road, they found themselves facing a black military vehicle and two men pointing ARs at them.

Keeping their hands in plain sight, the two brothers sat on their horses, waiting for the two military men to do something.

"You two boys ride over this way nice and slow," said one of the uniformed men.

Fred led his horse toward them, and Billy followed.

"Can I help you, sir?" Fred asked. He knew enough to be polite when someone was pointing a gun at him.

"What are you two doing out here?" the man asked.

"Huntin' turkey," Fred answered. He reached for the birds when the other man fired a shot, a bullet striking just in front of Tom's horse, spooking the animal and throwing Tom to the ground.

"I told you nice and slow," the first man said.

Fred sat up and slowly began to get up off the ground.

"Why don't you stay right there," the man said.

Fred didn't move.

The man who had shot at them came forward, his weapon still pointed at Fred.

Billy, not sure what to do, raised his hands slowly and sat still on his horse.

"Now tell me again, what are you doing out here?" the first man asked.

"Huntin' turkey," Fred answered.

"You got a license to hunt turkey," the military man asked.

"Don't need no damn license," Fred replied angrily. "There ain't no government to get one from."

"You're funny, boy," the man said. "See, we're here from the government."

Fred was confused and glanced at Billy, who was still sitting there, arms raised and saying nothing.

"I think we'll have to confiscate those turkeys. You're poaching, and that's a crime," the military man said.

"It ain't no crime to get food for your family," Fred spat.

"Watch your mouth, boy, show some respect," the man said calmly. "You on the horse, bring me those two birds you got and then go get the other two. Remember, we got this one here, so don't try anything stupid."

Billy did as ordered. He walked his horse over and dropped his two turkeys on the road by the man.

Then, he went and got Fred's horse, bringing it back. He took the two turkey from the horse and dropped those on the ground, too.

"What's your name, boy?" the man asked him.

"Billy, Billy Winston. This is my brother, Fred."

"You two know the Henrys?" the man asked.

"Never heard of 'em," Fred answered.

"I didn't ask *you*. I asked this one," the man said as he pointed his weapon at Billy.

"Like my brother said, we don't know any Henrys," Billy said.

"Well," the man said, "if you *suddenly* remember you do, tell them the government is here for them." The man reached down and picked up the birds, tossing them in the back of his vehicle. "You two get on your horses and get out of here. Oh, and we'll see you again real soon. You can't be up here anymore."

Fred stood up and got back on his horse.

Just as they started to ride away, the man said, "Wait a minute. Leave those guns here, too. You can't have those, either."

"We need these weapons to hunt for food," Fred said.

"Try fishing," the man said as he took the shotguns away from Fred and Billy. "Now ride off, the both of you. And don't forget, if you remember you know the Henrys, tell 'em we are coming for them."

Fred and Billy rode off at a walk.

After they were about twenty yards away, they kicked their horses into a gallop and rode quickly down the road. This was not going to sit well with their father.

***

Craig was on watch in the bunker again. Addie had come out to be with him, and the two of them were sitting inside, the cool air of the bunker giving them reason to sit close to each other. Craig had his arm around Addie as they leaned against the log wall while still having a good view of the road out front.

He and Addie were saying nothing to each other but enjoying the comfortable silence of each other's company.

John would be pretty mad that Addie was with him. If he caught them jabbering, he'd be double mad. But he didn't have to find out.

Craig heard the approaching vehicle coming down the road before he saw it. As it came into view, he immediately recognized it as a Hummer. However, this one was different. This didn't look like the ones Rahn had used. This vehicle was solid flat black. He reached for the TA-312 field phone that was sitting on a log next to him and cranked the handle.

"Hello," the voice on the other end answered. It sounded like Linda. "This is Craig in the bunker. Is my dad or Brian nearby?"

"Hold on," Linda said.

A few seconds later, he heard over the line. "What's up, Craig?" Dad asked.

"There's a black Hummer driving down the road. He isn't going fast, about 20 miles an hour, maybe."

"Keep an eye on them, son, and stay in the bunker. Do not confront them. Do you understand, Craig?"

"I do," Craig said, putting the receiver in the cradle. Looking at Addie, he said, "You should get back to your cabin."

***

Setting the phone in the cradle in the bag, I went running to find Brian and Rahn. I found Brian first as he headed toward the cabin.

"Where's Rahn?" I asked.

"I left him by the barn. What's up, Dad?" he asked.

"We might have company. I think Rahn's friends from Wausau are here." I didn't give him a chance to answer. I kept heading for the barn. He followed me.

As I approached the barn, I could see Rahn inside the bay, talking to a couple of his soldiers.

"Chris," I shouted.

He waved at me, said something to the soldiers, and came my way. As he got close, I said, "We have company."

"What kind of company?" he asked, wary.

"The kind that drives black HMWWVs," I said.

"Shit, that didn't take long. I wonder how they found us so fast. Your location wasn't in any of my reports."

"Most likely, your major. I met him once."

"He ain't my major anymore, John. Now he's one of the bad guys. Where did you see the HMWWV?"

"I didn't, Craig did. He said it was driving slow on the road out front."

"Hmmm… They don't know where we are?"

"That's my thought, too. I told Craig not to engage or confront them. We have the advantage right now, and we need that."

"Good idea. Those men are not gangbangers or criminal refugee bands. Those are trained soldiers. We won't surprise them like you have the others," Rahn said.

"More than likely, they want us to know they are here and that they have a good idea where we are," Brian interjected. "I think we send them a message that is hard to ignore."

"What do you got in mind, Chief?" Rahn asked.

"An ambush, but not here. More like in town. They know we are in Lake View, but they don't know exactly where. I say we take out a patrol, leave the bodies, and a note. Tell 'em to go back where they came from."

"They won't listen," Rahn said, shaking his head. "Wolfe came here with soldiers. Those are probably FEMA QRF, and they'll be like bloodhounds on a scent. They won't leave and will see casualties as a cost of doing business."

"Besides, Brian, we draw first blood and they now have an excuse to wreak holy hell on us and everyone else. It would legitimize them," I interjected.

"Then we make that cost very, very high for them," Brian said. "We find a way to get their attention, and get it good."

"Our people don't have those kind of skills, not against a trained force," I said.

Brian stared hard at me. "I won't use our people, Dad. I have trained soldiers here now."

"That's gonna take some getting used to," I replied. "Getting used to in a good way, but it will still take getting used to."

"Rahn and I'll plan something and then run it by you. You can pick it apart or say it's a go."

"Sure. I need a drink and a cigar," I said as I headed back to the cabin.

"Day drinking, Dad. That's not good for you," Brian said jovially.

I showed him my middle finger as I continued toward the cabin.

I walked inside, went to where my Rebel Yell was stashed and poured about four fingers into a glass. I grabbed a cigar and went to the porch.

After lighting it, I took a sip of my whiskey and leaned back in the chair. *This is getting complicated. I wish Carol was here. She could help me sort this out. Brian's in charge now, and I'm just "Dad." Probably a good thing. They're the professionals. They should be handling this. My skills are from another time. All I know is quick violence and some basic stuff. Between Brian and Rahn, those soldiers they lead are going to be brutal.*

That last thought saddened me. War is always brutal because if it isn't, you aren't doing it right. The brutality changes a person, and not always for the better. I didn't want my son to change.

The whiskey was calming me down, and I realized I had poured too much. I probably only needed about half of what I had. The cigar was different. I could easily solve all the world's problems with a cigar.

The creak of the door got my attention and drew

my eyes toward the sound. It was Linda, wearing an apron and smudged with patches of flour. It wouldn't be long before we started grinding the wheat berries I had stored for flour. We'd have to start thinking about growing our own, which was going to take more of the field. My having had all of this secluded acreage was becoming fortuitous.

"You look like you've been enjoying yourself," I said as she came onto the porch.

"Making bread," she replied. "You look like you're enjoying yourself, too. Day drinking, John?"

It sounded somehow different coming from her. I afelt remorseful because of how she said it to me. So soon after Carol and I couldn't believe a woman would affect me like that, but Linda was beginning to.

"I needed to think," I said, casting my eyes toward the porch floor, feeling a little embarrassed.

"I've heard whiskey makes men into geniuses," she replied, though not in a scolding way. It was obvious she was teasing me good-naturedly.

She came over and sat in the chair next to me. Reaching her hand over, she patted my arm and said, "What's got you so worried today, John?"

"We're getting ready to have trouble," I answered, not meeting her eyes.

"We have trouble every day. What makes today different?"

"It would appear that Rahn has people in the area looking for him. People trained to do that," I clarified.

"That's not sounding like normal trouble," she said. "That sounds like serious, we have a problem, trouble."

"Yep, dangerous trouble. The kind that people get hurt from, or worse. This time I think we'll see the 'or worse' part of that."

"We're in danger, aren't we?" she asked.

"I'm afraid so, and I'm concerned."

"That doesn't help make me feel any better, John. If you're concerned, it could be bad."

"I'm not going to lie to you, Linda, and I never will.

But, yeah, this time it's real serious."

"What are we going to do?"

"For now, the soldiers are going to deal with it. I'm sure the rest of us will have to get involved at some point, but they'll take on the bulk of what needs to be done."

"Should I let the others know?" she asked.

"Probably a good idea. Let them know that we are back in it again and that we'll need to be ready for casualties of any kind."

"Why can't we be allowed to live in peace?" she asked.

It didn't seem the question was necessarily directed at me, but I answered it anyway. "Some people just like to control others. Some people are cruel or naturally mean. A year ago, I came here, in part, to get away from all that. To be left alone, not bothered."

"And a small cabin build there," she interrupted. Her eyes showed that she understood the poem now that I had reiterated for her and why I came here.

"Yes, and that. I built the cabin not so small, though. It was good."

"We'll just have to make it good again," she said as she rose out of the chair. "Sometimes, bad things happen, and we have to face them before we can have good things again. Seems like we have to face some more bad before we can have good again."

I watched her as she went back inside the cabin, the creak and the slam-slam of the screen door signaling her departure.

I had to relight my cigar, and once I did that, I reached under the chair where I had placed my drink. I decided I really did need four fingers. Just as I swallowed the first sip, Rahn and Brian came up on the porch.

"We have an idea," Brian said.

"What is it?" I asked.

For the next few hours, we discussed what the idea was and how to make it work. The ladies came outside, shooed the kids away from us, and the others saw we were in an intense conversation and left us alone. We finished, and had a cold supper. In the next few days, a lot of things would be served cold. The cold, emotionless action of people pushed too far.

Chapter 14

"Remember, the storm is a good opportunity for the pine and the cypress to show their strength and their stability."

—Ho Chi Minh

The old man had to stretch himself as the horse plodded along the side of the road. Standing up slightly in the stirrups, he leaned back, his two hands nestled in his lower back for support. He had gray hair with a large bald spot on the crown, which he hid with a farm implement cap. He had tan overalls and a long sleeve t-shirt on that could use a good washing. Two younger men accompanied him, both dressed similarly. Charlie Winston, patriarch of the Winston family, and two of his three sons, Fred and Billy, were on a mission.

Fred and Billy had been accosted by "gubmint" troops, and Charlie was having none of that. He knew John Henry had connections with the soldiers, and that is where they were heading now, to see John Henry.

They had left before dawn, mostly to avoid the heat of the day, and while it was still morning, Charlie knew today would be warm, at least by his standards. "Gonna get hot today, boys," he said to his sons. "Might get to 80."

Fred and Billy made eye contact with each other and smiled briefly. Their dad's heat intolerance was legendary. All of the Winstons pretty much had lived a rustic life. They had the basics, but air conditioning was not one of those. As a result, when it got hot, Charlie let you know about it.

After another hour on horseback, the trio arrived at the entrance to the Henry place.

"Who's in the bunker?" Charlie yelled out.

"I am, Mr. Winston," Rick Stepanik yelled back.

"Well, let the people up at your cabin know that I'm here, son," Charlie replied as he led his horse up the drive, the two boys following him.

"Boys, we're going to be here a while…"

***

I was waiting for the Winstons on the porch as they rode up. One thing you can say about Charlie Winston, there is no hurry up in him. He and the horse just casually stepped up toward the cabin. His two sons had waved at me. Charlie didn't like to wave at anybody. It was just his nature.

"Morning, Charlie," I said as he started to dismount.

"Mornin', John," he groaned as he stepped to the ground, arched his back and bent forward. "I'm getting a bit long in the tooth for all this riding."

"Comes to us all in time," I replied. "Fred, Billy, why don't you come up on the porch, too." The two men did as I suggested, staying quiet and deferring to their father for any talking.

"Thank you for the pigs, Charlie," I began. "We sure will appreciate having them over the winter."

"You're a good neighbor, and I didn't mind sweetening the deal. Truth is, I have more pigs right now than I know what to do with. Might have to see about setting up some kind of store or trading post."

"That could be a good idea, Charlie. Be a good step toward turning things back to normal. So what brings you out here today. My end of the bargain isn't even growing yet." Of course, I was talking about the foals we had promised him in return.

"Fred and Billy had a run-in with some gubmint people yesterday. Took their days hunting from them and chased the boys away with those automatic rifles you people are so fond of. Took their shotguns, too."

As he finished his story, Rahn and Brian came up onto the porch, having just walked over from the barn.

"Mornin' Mr. Winston, Fred, Billie," Brian said. "This is First Sergeant Chris Rahn. He and I have put together a small group of soldiers to help us out up here."

"You're gonna need 'em," Charlie said. "The boys here already had a run-in."

"That right, Fred, Billy?" Brian asked.

"I didn't make it up, son," Charlie said before either of the brothers had a chance to reply.

"Sorry, Mr. Winston. I didn't mean to question your word. I wanted to hear what they saw," Brian replied.

Fred glanced at his father, and Charlie nodded his head, showing it was okay to proceed.

"Yeah, Brian, we did. Billy and me went hunting yesterday for turkey. Got two each, nice couple of Jakes and hens. Anyways, we was riding back, and there were these two men in a black vehicle, like one of those." He pointed at Rahn's HMWWV parked under a tree thirty feet away. "They were pointing ARs at us, shot at us, and took the turkeys and our shotguns."

"Yeah, and my shotgun was a good Benelli, too," Billy interjected.

"That's an expensive shotgun," Rahn said. "How'd you get that? I can't even afford one."

"Casino over on the Rez," Billy said. "I know a lot of the boys over there, and they had a raffle. I won." There was something about the way he said "I won" that told me there was much more to the story, and probably something I didn't want to learn more about at this time.

"Mr. Henry, they said to tell you they was coming for you," Fred added.

"They aren't just coming for me, Fred," I said. "They are coming for all of us. They want to put us in camps, or worse."

"Yeah, they said something about how we can't be up here anymore," Fred continued. "We ain't going anywhere."

"We aren't, either," I said.

About that time, the door creaked. Donna and Nancy came out carrying the coffee pot and some cups. "John, where are your manners? You didn't offer these fine people any coffee," Donna said.

No one said no to the coffee, even though we said we had no cream or sugar. We still had it, but by silent agreement, we were determined to keep it for ourselves.

"You should get you some milk cows," Charlie said. "Plenty of 'em around needing a home."

"We should," I said. I didn't tell him about the two we had in the barn that we had found on one of our scavenging trips. I had about a hundred pounds of sugar in the basement, and when that ran out, we had raw honey. There were two natural hives I knew of on the property.

"Thank you, missy," Charlie said as he took a steaming cup from Donna. "I don't put anything but sugar in my coffee anyways. This will do just fine."

"John," Charlie said, "you think they'll be back to get us?"

"I think they will, Charlie, I think they'll try hard to run us off and into that camp in Wausau," I replied.

"I ain't going and none of mine are going, either," Charlie said firmly as he glanced at Fred and Billy.

"We are here to help make sure that doesn't happen, Mr. Winston," Rahn interjected. "I left because they were forcing me to do things that were just wrong. *I'm following orders* is a poor excuse, and I won't use it."

"Seems to me these FEMA people are no different than those people you're talking about, soldier. My daddy fought them, guess maybe I might have to, too."

"I fear it's coming to that, Charlie," I said.

***

Elias Wolfe and the QRF were getting ready to increase the pressure. Four teams, using four of the vehicles they had, would begin searching for people who had not followed the state's orders to assemble in Wausau or surrendered to the teams that had been sent out to bring them in.

Captain Jamison's idea was simple. Send out the teams, harass and arrest civilians who they otherwise would not have bothered with, and create enough of a stir to cause the Henrys to react. It would also keep the men busy and on edge, ensuring that nothing came as a surprise to them as they went about their mission.

"We'll have these four teams driving in and around Lake View going all the way to the Menominee Reservation. Any small groups of people they pick up, they can zip tie them, and put them in the bed of the Hummer or in the rear seats. Either way, we start rounding people up, and we'll draw them out," Roy explained to Elias.

"Just picking up people may not be enough," Elias commented. "You might have to get rough. We had a lot of people from Lake View and the surrounding area voluntarily give themselves up. There aren't that many holding out. Those that *are* will be the hard cases, in my opinion. They won't go easy."

"I told the teams, if necessary, they could burn down houses, food stores, shoot farm animals, whatever they needed to do to get the point across." Roy chuckled. "Let the boys have a bit of fun."

"Oh, I think that would do it," Wolfe remarked. "Anything to stop this rebellion before it gets too far out of hand." *And save my place in the new ruling class.*

***

Brian and Rahn had made a sand table of the town, placing it in the large bay area of the barn. The buildings, roads, landmarks, and other large objects that could be used for both cover and concealment were all identified. Blocks of wood, rocks, or lines in the sand indicated each object.

The plan was simple enough. They were to wait for the QRF patrol to enter town, and use debris from the fire that was set by looters last year, bushes, and anything else they could find to camouflage the HMMWV with the turret-mounted SAW. Once the QRF patrol was in range, they were to disable it with the SAW and send the occupants back to their base in Antigo on foot. That was a not so pleasant 25 miles away.

"Do your best not to kill them," Rahn said.

"Why?" Specialist Hart asked. "They have every intention of doing that to us."

Brian could see the red starting to creep up Rahn's neck. The first sergeant didn't like his orders being questioned, especially in a briefing.

"If we kill them, we escalate the situation. If we kill first, then we are at fault, and not them. So, if at all possible, no QRF should be killed in action," Brian explained firmly.

"Mistakes happen, Chief. We can't guarantee that one of them won't accidentally get killed."

"HART!" Rahn said a bit loudly. "There better not be any fucking accidents out there or *you'll* be an accident. Am I clear?"

"Crystal, First Sergeant," Hart replied.

"Any other questions?" Rahn asked.

The men sat silently, and not one said a word.

"Okay, tomorrow at zero five-thirty, Hart, you and Owens will go out until noon. Specialist Myer, at eleven-thirty hours, you will depart here with PFC Klotz and enter the town slowly. You will put eyes on the road and Specialist Hart and Owens. Once you determine you can trade off without being seen, you will relieve them, at which time Hart and Owens, you will return here. Myer and Klotz, you will remain in place until eighteen hundred." He glanced at the men.

"At that time, you will put eyes on the town and ensure that you are not being observed. You will then withdraw here," Rahn instructed. "If nothing happens, then we send out new teams the next day and do it all over again. We do that until we accomplish the mission or come up with something else."

"Yes, First Sergeant," the men replied.

"Chief, you got anything to add?" Rahn asked.

"Yes, thank you, Rahn. Men, once again, the infantry gets the dirty end of the stick. I know I'm sending you out there, and you are to shoot at our enemy but not hit them. Sucks, I know. We have to make them understand we want to be left alone, and they are to leave. We can't go getting into a firefight with an armed force bigger than us and with similar training. The first sergeant tells me you are good soldiers. I believe in you and believe you are."

He looked at each man in turn. "Now, when the first sergeant and I were fighting Hajis in the surge, we were mountaineers. We were the 10th Mountain Division, and our motto was 'Right of the Line and Climb to Glory!' You men all come from different Wisconsin National Guard units. We need something to bring us together, so our motto is 'Climb to Glory.'"

"Chief, is that because we ain't got nobody to our left?" asked PFC Bennet.

The men all laughed at the very real words. Brian let them have their laugh. It was good for morale and helped relieve tension.

"Bennet," Brian said, "we pretty much are flopping in the breeze out there, so we are the left, the right, and everything in between. CLIMB TO GLORY!" Brian said.

The soldiers all jumped to their feet and chanted, "HOOAH, CLIMB TO GLORY, SIR!"

"Dismissed," Brian ordered.

The men slowly filtered away, leaving Rahn and

Brian alone. Brian traced his finger through the sandbox. Rahn got a little closer, and in a low voice, said, "Climb to Glory, Brian. That the best you could do?"

"It was better than what I was originally thinking," Brian said.

"What's that?" Rahn asked.

"Please don't let us fuck up."

***

The early morning light was just beginning to peak when Specialist Hart and Private Bill Owens started up the HMWWV. Owens was in the turret. It was locked in place, and he had his arm resting on the SAW. Hart pulled rank and said he was driving.

Rahn and Brian were there and had already reviewed the ammo load that the two men had with them, listened to the men recite their instructions, including the no enemy casualties requirement.

Both men were dressed in ACUs and wore ACHs or Advanced Combat Helmets without the night vision goggles or NVGs. They each had an M9 pistol and an AR in addition to the SAW that Owens would man.

"You men be careful out there," Brian said. "I want you both back."

"We got this, Chief," Hart remarked, and with that the HMMWV rolled forward and headed for town.

"I hope Hart keeps his cool," Rahn said.

"He will," Brian replied. "What are you worried about?"

"He caught some of those FEMA guys abusing a high school girl, and he damn near killed them. It took everything I could to keep him from going into the slammer. He hates them."

***

Wolfe and Jamison stood by as the four teams rolled

out of the armory parking lot. Each HMMWV had two black-clad QRF members who carried their personal weapons. The teams were cutting up and bragging about all the damage they were going to do.

Jamison walked around, and like a cheerleader, encouraged their enthusiasm, bringing it to a high pitch.

As each vehicle drove by, he pumped his arm up and down, his hand balled in a fist, encouraging them further.

"I wish you'd let me go with one of them, Roy," Wolfe said as the last vehicle pulled out. "I need to be out there."

"Those are my men, Elias, and they know what to do. They don't need us with them until it's time. Besides, if they take casualties, we are still here uninjured and alive. Let them soften those people up before we take our turn. You'll get your success."

"Yeah, but if they run into Rahn and the Henrys, two men isn't enough. They'll need our experience and firepower."

"You ain't Rambo, Elias, and neither am I. If they get hit, that will inspire the men more. We can use that to turn these men into exactly what we need—a horde of angry warriors who won't let anything stop them. Besides, if one of them gets hurt or killed, we have our reason to engage without mercy."

"I guess so, but I still wish I was going with them. I deserve to go with them. I know this area better than any of you."

"Relax, Elias. You'll get your turn. Let's go get some chow," Jamison said and went back inside the armory.

Elias watched them go and then, with a shrug, turned and went inside, too.

Some coffee and breakfast might be just what I need to settle me down. I still think I should have gone with them. They need my experience and leadership.

***

Owens and Hart pulled in next to the rubble that had been a Quik Mart. Finding a spot to park their vehicle and have a good view of the road took a few minutes. Next, they spent about a half-hour bringing burnt timbers and branches with dried leaves to conceal their position. They knew it didn't have to be obscured entirely, just enough for the element of surprise before they opened up with the SAW.

Owens took the first watch from the turret. He flipped the latch to allow it to move freely, locked and loaded the Saw, and, using the binoculars, began to watch down the road.

"I'm gonna rack out for a while, Owens," Hart said. "Wake me if you hear or see anything. I don't want to miss the action."

"No problem, just don't snore. It might let them know we're here."

"I don't snore," Hart replied.

"The hell you don't, you can wake the dead."

"At ease, Private."

"Yes, Specialist," Owens said with exaggerated sarcasm.

Hart curled up in the driver's seat while Owens began his watch.

Nothing was happening.

Then, Owens noticed some movement alongside the road, across from them that grabbed his attention.

Damn.

It was only a doe looking for breakfast. *Might have to come back and get you.*

Owens continued to look through the binoculars, seeing nothing. After a while, he set them down. *I'll hear them before I see them.*

The low rumble of an HMWWV sounded in the distance.

"Hart," Owens whispered.

The Specialist continued to sleep.

"Hart," Owens said a little louder.

The sleeping soldier didn't respond. Seeing no other option, Owens kicked him, which immediately woke up the sleeping man.

"What the fuck," Hart exclaimed.

"I hear something," Owens said. "Sounds like a Hummer."

Collecting himself, Hart picked up his M4 and check pressed it to make sure a round was chambered.

They were ready. Owens had pulled back the cocking handle on the SAW, and the weapon was ready to fire.

The soft rumble of the approaching vehicle got louder and louder. Hart had exited the vehicle and stood alongside the engine cowling, his M4 against his shoulder as he used the hood of the vehicle as a support.

It wasn't long before the approaching vehicle came into view. The black FEMA HMWWV was now in full sight.

"Take out the engine, Owens," Hart said. "I'll watch for anyone exiting the vehicle."

Owens felt his mouth go dry as the vehicle came closer. No one else was in the road. Still, his hands were getting clammy and his entire body was tense.

"Now, Owens," Hart said.

Owens froze up.

"Owens, FIRE!" Hart yelled.

The young private pulled the trigger. Ratatat, Ratatatat, Ratatat, Ratatatat.

Owens put three and four round bursts into the engine cowling of the black HMWWV.

The vehicle slid to a stop, steam rising from the engine. Two side doors of the vehicle flew open and black-clad men exited from each side.

The two men shot back at Hart and Owens.

Bullets bounced off of both HMWWVs, some penetrating into the bodies of the vehicles and beyond.

"Owens, get on the radio and call base. Tell them we are engaged," Hart shouted.

Owen dropped down from the turret and grabbed the handheld radio off of the seat. He could here Hart returning fire in three round bursts as the FEMA guys continued to fire at them.

"Base... Base, this is Scout One, over," Owens

yelled into the radio. "Base… Base, this is Scout One, over."

"Scout One this is Base, over," the voice sounded like Chief Henry.

"Base, this is Scout One. We are engaged, over," Owens said.

"SITREP, Scout One, over," Brian replied.

"Base, one enemy vehicle immobilized. Two, I say again, two enemy combatants actively returning fire, over."

"Scout One, hang in there. On our way, out."

"Base, Roger. Scout One out," Owens replied. Dropping the radio, he raised back up into the turret only to immediately catch a piece of shrapnel in his cheek, which tore a long gouge across his face.

"SHIT!" he screamed. "I'm hit."

"Where?" Hart shouted back.

"My face. Everything works though," Owens yelled as he continued to return fire.

***

"RAHN!" Brian shouted, bursting out the front door of the cabin, his feet barely touching the porch floor or steps. Leaping from the porch and landing on the ground, he never lost stride. Dashing across the yard toward the barn, he shouted again, "RAHN!"

First Sergeant Rahn came out of the barn with Specialist Myer and PFC Klotz.

"MOUNT UP, WE HAVE ENGAGEMENT," Brian yelled.

Rahn dropped his coffee cup and ran into the barn, grabbing his improved load bearing equipment with only the assault pack and hydration system.

Myer and Klotz already had their ACHs on, the chin straps secured. Both kept their weapons in the HMWWV they were to ride in.

Brian jumped into the front passenger seat, Klotz and Rahn in the back of the cab where Klotz stood up into the turret with the SAW.

Myer took the position of driver. Each of the men barely had a chance to get into their seats before Myer pushed on the accelerator and sped out of the barnyard toward the road. The tires grabbed and squealed as soon as they hit the paved surface of the road as Myer raced toward town.

Brian glanced over at the speedometer and saw it was almost 60 MPH. "Don't kill us before we get there, Myer," Brian shouted.

Turning in his seat, Brian said to Rahn, "Owens reported contact, and I could hear three-round bursts close by with more rapid-fire being directed at them."

"How many enemy combatants?" Rahn asked.

"Owens said two. They have disabled their vehicle, so the only way those two FEMA guys are getting away is on foot. I'm hoping our showing up will make them beat feet in retreat."

"That'd be nice. Any casualty reports?" Rahn asked, holding tight to a handhold grip.

"He didn't say. We'll find out soon enough," Brian replied. Now that they were getting closer, he could hear the sound of gunshots, the bursts from the SAW being the most distinctive.

"Klotz, when we get there, I want you to put suppressing fire on that black HMWWV," Rahn shouted up into the turret.

"Roger, First Sergeant."

"Klotz, no anti-personnel fire unless me or the chief gives the order."

"Roger that, First Sergeant."

The HMWWV continued to speed toward the old Quik Mart. It took a minute or two before Brian could see the black HMWWV with what appeared to be smoke rising from its hood. He could also see the Scout One Hummer and someone, he assumed Hart, behind the vehicle shooting toward the black FEMA vehicle.

Owens was hunched over the SAW masterfully, putting three and four round bursts toward the FEMA combatants.

"Okay, Klotz, fire away," Rahn yelled up into the turret.

RATATATAT, RATATATAT, RATATATAT! Klotz put suppressing fire into the black vehicle hood and engine compartment, ensuring that it wasn't going anywhere.

The arrival of Brian, Rahn, and the rest of Scout Two caused a brief lull from the other engaged parties.

Owens waved his arms over his head, pumped his fist, and then hunched back over his SAW, continuing the fight.

Hart had come around to the rear of the vehicle after grabbing the radio from the front seat and called, "Scout Two, this is Scout One, over."

Brian replied, "Scout One, Scout two, over."

"Glad you're here, Scout Two, this is a standoff. Neither of us are going anywhere," Hart said.

"Let's see if we can run these SOBs off then, Scout One," Brian replied. He ordered Myer to stop the vehicle. With Klotz in the turret continuing to suppress fire, Brian, Myer, and Rahn took cover behind their HMWWV and put fire onto the area where they thought the two FEMA combatants were.

It didn't take long for fire coming toward Scout Two to diminish, and Brian could see two black-clad men running away.

"CEASE FIRE," Brian shouted. "CEASE FIRE!"

The shooting came to a standstill, and along with it, that awkward silence.

"Klotz, stay alert," Rahn said.

Brian and Rahn walked over to Hart and Owens. It was then they noticed Owens' blood-covered face.

"Owens, you've been shot," Brian remarked.

"Oh, no, Sir. It's just a ricochet of shrapnel," Owens said.

"Go see Specialist Myer and get it looked at," Brian directed.

"Yes, sir," Owens replied and jogged off toward the Scout Two-vehicle and Specialist Myer.

"Good job, Hart," Rahn said as Hart joined them.

"Thank you, First Sergeant," Hart said. His hands began to tremble as the adrenalin in his body started to dissipate. "Mind if I sit down?"

"Go right ahead," Brian said. "Now tell us how this all went down."

***

"Captain Jamison," the QRF team member stood at the door of what had been Major Wolfe's office as stated from the sign still on the door.

"Yes, what is it?" Jamison asked, looking up from an old magazine he was scanning through.

"Captain, we've got radio traffic that isn't ours."

"Okay, and…" Jamison replied testily.

"Sir, their call signs are Scout One and Base. They said they were engaged."

Jamison dropped his magazine and instantly made eye contact with Wolfe, who had been playing with a pile of paperclips on the desk. The two men hopped to their feet.

"Say that again?" Jamison directed.

"Their call signs are Scout One and Base. They said they were engaged."

"Com Center, NOW," Jamison yelled as he pointed out the door and indicated the Communications Center. The FEMA soldier turned and dashed out the door, with Jamison and Wolfe behind him.

The three men almost collided as they entered the communications center.

"That radio over there, Sir," the FEMA soldier said, pointing toward a radio against a bare wall. An operator sat in front of it and had a notebook on the desk, which he was writing on.

"Have there been any further messages?" Jamison asked.

"Yes, sir," the operator remarked.

Reading from his notes, the operator said, "This is what I transcribed Sir, verbatim. 'Base, this is Scout One. One enemy vehicle immobilized. Two, I say again, two enemy combatants actively returning fire, over. Scout One, hang in there, on our way, out, Base. Roger, Scout One, out.'

"And then, just a short while ago there was this, 'Scout Two, this is Scout One, over. Scout One, Scout Two, over. Glad you're here, Scout Two, this is a standoff. Neither of us are going anywhere. Let's see if we can run these SOBs off then, Scout One.' That's it, Sir, no further transmissions."

"Thank you. Let me know immediately if you hear anything more," Jamison said. Motioning with his head toward the door, Jamison followed Wolfe out into the hall.

"Besides that we may have lost one of our vehicles, it seems like we may have learned Henry and Rahn are together," he said.

"How do you figure that?" Wolfe asked.

"Just making a conclusion from the transmission." Jamison gave him a hard look. "Go back in there and have them divert one of the other teams to find our two guys, and if possible, assess the damage. We have our little incident, and now we can use it to our advantage. Radio the other two teams to be more aggressive. Let them know a team was attacked, and the vehicle destroyed. Give them no other information; just say you don't know."

Wolfe nodded his head and went back inside the Communications Center with a smile on his face and anger in his eyes. *This is all working out just fine.*

Chapter 15

*"A time of innocence can be an unsettling calm
before a ferocious storm."*

—Brian Henry

"One of our teams has been attacked. You are now ordered to aggressively seek out insurgents and render them harmless," the voice over the radio speaker said.

"Roger, Base Camp," the black-uniformed FEMA soldier said into the radio. "I guess we have our orders. What to do, what to do," he said to his partner.

"Let's stay on this road and see what we find," the other FEMA soldier said.

"Somewhere along here, we will cross into the Menominee Reservation. We ain't supposed to go there."

"Whatever, dude, we're ordered to stir shit up, and this is where we are… Well, hello there. Seek, and ye shall find."

In a field off to their right, the FEMA soldier observed two men herding dairy cows on foot. "Let's go chase some cows," he said to his partner.

"Chase cows?" his partner, who was driving the HMWWV, asked.

"Yup, cows." The first soldier pointed out into the field.

"Well, hell, let's go!" the driver shouted as he turned off to the right, knocking down a fence and heading

208

straight for the cows and two men on foot.

It didn't take them long to hit a cow, almost hit one of the men, and scatter the small herd.

They left the field as fast as they entered it and drove west.

***

Brian, along with Scout One and Scout Two, returned home, having seen no other FEMA vehicles on the road.

Rahn took Owens up to the cabin to have his cheek looked at and stitched up, the cut being long and a bit deep. And then he went off to find Brian.

Linda was there waiting for them. She sat Owens down on the edge of the porch where the light was better.

She dressed the wound, but the only pain killer she had was topical lidocaine. It worked, though not as well as the injectable kind. To distract him and take his mind off of the poking and pulling, Linda asked him about his home.

"I'm from Rhinelander originally," Owens said. "A few years ago, my parents retired and moved to Florida. I'm an only child. I haven't heard from them since all of this started, not that we were all that close anyway."

"I'm sure once this is all over you'll be able to find them. I'll bet the first sergeant will let you go," she said. "You seem like a good person. Your heart's in the right place, and I can't see him telling you no."

"Maybe you could help me talk to him?" Owens replied. "A pretty lady like you might win him over."

"That's sweet, thank you," she said. Then, patting his uninjured cheek softly, she hugged him and said he was all fixed up.

Private Owens walked away, his cheeks slightly red. Seeing Johnson coming towards the cabin, he said, "I think I'm in love."

"Don't get your hopes up, Owens. I think she's spoken for."

"Damn," he muttered.

***

Overhearing Johnson and Owens' conversation, Rahn laughed. He saw Brian talking to John and went over to join them.

"Hi, Chris," John said. "Sounds like everything went well today. How's the soldier, Owens, isn't it?"

"It went as well as could be expected. As for the soldier, yes, it is Owens. He's in love and has a broken heart."

"Oh?" John said, raising a brow. "With who?"

"Linda. I told him to forget about it."

"He must've took it hard if that broke his heart," Brian said.

"Nah," Rahn grinned. "I told him she was spoken for."

"By who?" John asked.

"You," Rahn said, then quickly left, heading toward the barn.

John could hear his laughter as he walked away.

"What the hell, Rahn. That's not funny."

He raised his arm and wiggled his fingers as he continued to walk away.

***

Three FEMA vehicles returned to the armory. One team had picked up the two QRF guys who were in the hot, slow process of making the long walk back to Antigo. Dirty, tired, and angry, the two walkers were in no mood for the jovial harassment they received from their teammates.

Captain Jamison put an end to their antics and called them all in front of him. He had Wolfe join him as he addressed the men.

"We got bloodied today, although thankfully no one was hurt. It won't be like that the next time. Some of you had some fun, I heard. Chasing cows in a field is fun but not exactly the kind of fun I sent you out there for. Only one team brought in prisoners, and they don't amount to shit. Next time I send you out, I want prisoners, I want arson, and I want havoc," he said.

"Yes, sir," the men replied.

"Now go get some chow. Nobody goes out tomorrow. I want to put something together that will give them shock and awe like they've never even experienced."

The men shuffled off, dejected but not defeated.

"Havoc, Roy?" Wolfe asked.

"Havoc, Elias. As in Cry Havoc, and let slip the dogs of war. That's Shakespeare in case you didn't know."

Wolfe nodded. "I like that. I like that a lot."

"You'll like it, even more, when I tell you that it's time."

"Time for what?"

"It's time for you to go out with them. You and me. We'll lead the action. This time from the front."

An evil grin spread across Wolfe's face and would have been funny were it not for the maliciousness in his eyes.

***

Brian, Rahn, and I decided it was a good idea to send out a roving patrol every day. We had Sam join us because he was our HAM radio operator and kept us up to date. Sam said he could maintain radio contact with them, as well as keep us updated on any radio traffic from FEMA or elsewhere. It was important that we keep any intruders away from the homestead. We were not set up to fight anyone here, and I didn't want to do that and risk everything anyway.

We limited the patrols to a 7 mile circumference, which was the optimal distance for our radios. Rahn had radios in his vehicles, but for the moment, we were suspicious of using them. The FEMA people had the same radios, and we could occasionally catch parts of their transmissions. Believing they could do the same to ours, plus it was possible they had stronger antennas, we decided to stick with the handhelds.

We also thought that our ability to react to a call that was no more than 7 miles out was a better option, too. The patrols were to act as a screening force and deny any hostile element to get closer than 3 miles from our home. I felt we could be successful with that.

We put some of the soldiers to work with building the new cabins.

They grumbled at first. Donna and Nancy heard their grumbles and complained to me and Brian.

I laughed, which didn't go over very well. Brian told them that soldiers aren't happy unless they *are* grumbling. The work continued, and with the help of Sajan and Gary, both having become experts at log cabins, the work was going smoothly.

Then I got called to the cabin by Linda, due to a call from the bunker.

"It's Craig, we have visitors," she explained.

I picked up the phone and said, "Craig, what's up?"

"I have two men out here on horseback. They're from the Rez. They say they know you and want to talk to you."

"I'll be there in a minute," I said. I hung up the phone and headed for the door.

Linda stopped me. "John, is it trouble?"

"No," I said. "Not this time, I don't think."

A few minutes later, I was at the bunker. There, talking jovially with Craig, was Peter Corn, a good friend of mine from the Menominee Reservation. The other man I did not recognize. Peter and I were both retired U.S. Army and had once served together in the same platoon many years ago. Our both being from Wisconsin sealed our friendship. Interestingly, we had said we'd never return to the state, yet here we were.

"Peter, you're looking old. How the hell are you?" I shouted.

He hopped off his horse and walked over to me.

I stuck out my hand.

He slapped it away, said, "Bull shit," and hugged me. It had been at least three years since we last saw each other, and that had been, of all things, to protest the logging operation that was now providing the logs that I was using to build my cabins.

"John Henry, it's good to see you, my friend. It has been too long," he said.

"What brings you off the Rez?" I asked. Peter and I had a very straight forward relationship. We came from a time and place where being oversensitive was nonsense, and honesty was everything. Neither of us offended easily, and because we were brothers in arms, we'd die for each other.

"We've had some trouble that I understand is your fault," Peter said.

"My fault?" I replied. "What the hell did I do now?"

We both laughed at the reference to eternal guilt.

"We had visitors yesterday. Some of those FEMA guys. They drove around one of our farms, killed a couple of milk cows, scared others into probably not producing milk for a while, and scared two of our young men half to death."

"I've got nothing to do with FEMA, Peter," I said. "Those assholes are after me, but I have nothing to do with them."

"So I've heard, but we got caught up in it. They just became our problem instead of just your problem."

"I'm both happy and sad to hear that, Peter," I replied. "I wish none of us had to deal with this, but I guess it is what it is. I'm glad you're here, Brother."

"I hear ya', John. We can't let them destroy our way of life up here."

"Where are my manners? Who is your friend?" I asked.

"Yeah, my manners suck, too. John, this is Joseph Grignon. Don't call him Joe. He doesn't like that." Peter chuckled.

I went over to the man, still sitting on his horse, and

stuck out my hand. He took it, and I said, "Pleased to meet you, Joseph."

"Likewise," he answered.

"Joseph doesn't say much," Peter said. "He's that silent Indian you read about."

"No shit," I said with a bemused tone.

"No shit," Peter said.

"C'mon up to the cabin. I have whiskey and cigars."

"You haven't changed at all, John Henry." Peter handed the reins to Craig, and said, "Here, hold my horse,"

I found it humorous but didn't laugh, as together we walked up to the cabin.

Joseph dismounted, gave his reins to Craig, said nothing, and followed behind us a few feet.

For the next few hours, Peter and I sat on the porch, caught up about the last three years, talked about our common problems, and what we could do about them. When he got up on his horse to leave, I felt a deep sadness. It had been a long time for us, but his being here made me realize just how important he was to me and my life here.

He said he was going to add to our force. The Rez had over a hundred able-bodied people that Peter said he could trust. He would send us ten immediately to do scouting and lookout work. Some of the others on the Rez still experienced the common problems that were on all reservations—drug and alcohol abuse.

Next, we were going to figure out how to incorporate them into our scout patrols. They would be on horseback, which would give them greater mobility, and as I pointed out, would keep all the action in my part of the woods and well away from Peter's.

Speed would be the real issue, as their scouts would have to be very old school.

Peter said they could handle that. "Indians have been sneakin' and peekin' in these woods for a thousand years. We know how to do that."

Because the FEMA people were in Antigo and the Henry homestead was between Antigo and the Rez,

Peter and I thought it would be best to house the patrols at my place. They'd keep the horses in my pasture, and by getting to know Rahn and Brian's men, it would help them all work better together.

Eventually, and that meant sooner rather than later, PFC Bennet and a couple of the other guard members would have time to rebuild a few of the motorcycles they had scavenged from the field by Carol's place. The cycles would give us both speed and increased mobility for the patrols we'd send out.

Things were beginning to fall into place. All we needed was time.

Dusk was fast approaching, so I decided to take a walk out into the field. The sound of crickets was everywhere. The smell of dry grass and the cool damp starting to roll out of the woods was a smell I was both familiar with and quite comfortable. My walk led me to Carol's grave. Next to her, Grady rested. We had marked both graves with simple wooden crosses that had their name and years they were among us.

I stood there, for I don't know how long, and remembered. I remembered the first time I met Carol, and how she made me a hamburger in her diner, how she spent time with Craig as he was growing up. I recalled our many conversations and the teasing over which was the better branch of service. I remembered the private times we had. And I remembered Carol, the first woman who had ever returned to me what I gave to her. My first successful relationship. For the first time, I didn't cry though I still missed her.

The voice behind me startled me a bit. "John…"

I turned and saw it was Linda. "I don't mean to intrude," she said.

"That's okay." *You aren't intruding at all.* The truth was I was glad to see her. I wasn't sure why I felt that way, but I was just glad to see her.

"I want to talk to you. I heard about the joke today, about you, that poor Owens and me."

"It angered me, too," I quickly added. "He shouldn't have said that."

"I don't know how I feel. That's why I wanted to talk to you. Do you claim me as yours, John? Am I spoken for in your mind?" Her direct tone was hard to decipher. Was she mad or just being Linda.

"I would never presume to even think something like that, Linda. I don't see things that way unless…"

"Unless what, John?"

"Unless it's by mutual consent, and shit, that makes me sound like a lawyer."

"I understand, and thank you. I'm not property, and I'm not a child. I will choose who I am with."

I reached my hand out, and she placed hers in mine. It seemed to be an automatic response to a gesture. "You're a good person. I do like you. I simply don't know."

"Don't know what?" she asked.

Avoiding her question, I said, "You have nice hands."

"I have stubby fingers, and my hands are rough."

"No, you have nice hands. The kind of hands that tell a simple yet honest story. These are the hands of someone who is not fake; these are the hands of someone who is everything you see and nothing more. You work with these hands, aren't afraid to get them dirty. The roughness is a symbol of the real and honest work that makes up life. There's no fancy manicure or hand treatment here. Just the hands of a genuine person who does simple, honest things. The honest hands of someone who does real and necessary work. The hands of someone who does the things that really matter in life. They are nice hands."

"Yeah, right," she said, her eyes cast down in a way that I feared I might have made her feel uncomfortable.

"I like your hands," I said as I let go of them. "I didn't mean to embarrass you," I added awkwardly.

"You didn't. The compliment was unexpected," Linda said. "You're a good man, John Henry."

"That's twice today someone called me by my full name and I wasn't in trouble," I replied.

We shared the laugh.

"It's starting to get dark; we should head back," I said.

"Yes, it is," she agreed. We walked toward the cabin side by side, and pushed through the tall grass, inches apart.

At first, her pace took her far out in front of me. "Are you in a hurry?" I asked.

"Sorry, I walk fast. A bad habit, I guess."

She stopped and waited for me to catch up. We headed back to the cabin, once again side by side, only this time, she walked more slowly. We didn't speak the whole way back, but we made eye contact several times.

She has pretty eyes, too.

***

Morning arrived, and I was where I always was when the sun rose—sitting in my chair on the porch. King and Max not far away. I was alone with my thoughts as the world awakened. I watched a cottontail nibbling at the clover near the edge of the barnyard. Most likely, a rabbit Mike had missed in his daily hunting. He had enlisted Linda's boys, Caleb and Ethan, in his daily hunts. The three of them had become deadly for rabbits and good for the stew pot. So good that many of us were starting to get a little tired of eating rabbit.

The cottontail left, the morning birds stopped their singing, and the noise of human activity started to pick up in the house. I could hear breakfast being made. Sadly, it wasn't pig killing time, so we still didn't have bacon. But that was only a matter of time.

The coffee I brought out with me, save a few drops in the bottom of the cup, was gone. I rose and headed indoors for a fresh cup.

Nancy had come downstairs, and Linda came over from the cabin she now had with her boys. They were helping Donna make pancakes with dried apples.

We chatted a few minutes about nothing important—

the garden, the weather, and little else. It was nice to have a normal, civilized conversation.

That all ended abruptly when Sam came in from the back door. Bursting into the room, he said, "John, come with me. I have someone on the radio for you."

"Who?" I asked.

"Come with me, John. We haven't much time."

"Who is it?" I insisted as I set my cup on the counter.

We left the kitchen and let the door close behind us. As we walked across the yard toward the barn, I asked again, "Who is it, Sam?"

"Major Wolfe," he said grimly.

We went up to the loft, and I sat in front of the radio. I picked up the handset, depressed the key, and said, "This is Henry, what do you want, Wolfe?"

"Is that you, Henry?" the voice on the other end said.

"That's what I said," I replied.

"This is Major Elias Wolfe," the voice said.

"That's nice. Your boys make it home, okay?"

Wolfe laughed. "I'm coming for you, Henry. I'm coming for you, that traitor Rahn, all of you. I'm going to destroy you all. You'll dance on a rope when we get done with you."

"That's nice, Wolfe. Anything else I need to worry about before I have breakfast?"

"You're all dead, Henry. Every one of you is dead…"

I looked at Sam before I set down the microphone. I didn't appreciate threats to my family.

"I'm growing to really hate that man," I said.

"He seems to have gained a bit of an ego. More than the one Rahn described," Sam answered.

"A dangerous ego, Sam. Something made him change, and what that is, I don't care. We'll need to deal with him, take him out most likely."

"We're really at war, aren't we?" Sam asked.

"I'm afraid so, buddy. A civil war. An ugly civil war," I replied.

"Not like you haven't seen that before, John. I know about Central America. I know what you told me."

"That's why I'm worried, Sam. I know. I think Brian and Rahn know, too. I'm not certain everybody else does. That worries me as much as what I'm afraid this will all turn in to."

Epilogue

The day was waning, and the two men sat by the firepit relaxing. It seemed that they relaxed every day. Neither of them was old, and in fact, neither was out of their thirties. They were just tired. Life had been hard these last few years, and after all of the struggle, it seemed peace was at hand. They intended to enjoy it.

Each man lit a cigar and leaned back in the Adirondack style chairs that surrounded the fire pit. As had become customary, the young girl joined them after they had sat there for a bit.

"Hello, sweetie," one of the men said. His brown beard bobbed up and down as he spoke.

"You promised to tell me more about my grandpa," she said, her tone demanding.

"You're awful young to be so demanding," the bearded one said. "If your grandpa was here, he'd probably swat you for it."

"Why?" she asked.

"He'd say you're rude."

"Damnit, that's not right," she said.

The bearded man said, "Don't blaspheme, sweetie."

"I'm sorry, it just makes me so mad. You know all about him, and I just wanna learn more."

"Well, of course, I know all about your grandpa. He was my dad."

"Then, tell me about him. I want to know. My dad says I'm just like him."

"My uncle is right. You *are* just like him, sweetie. Let me tell you the rest of the story. Sit down here, and I'll tell you more about your grandpa."

220

About the Author

D.M. Herrmann is a retired soldier, having spent twenty years in the U.S. Army. He has authored three fiction novels under the pseudonym Evan Michael Martin. *Their Star Is Their World* is the second novel in the John Henry Chronicles series. He lives in Wisconsin.